# Thank You

*Nine Kinds of Trouble is a collection of short stories written over a period of years and published in various print magazines, ezines, and anthologies. Thank you for your purchase. I hope you enjoy reading these stories as much as I enjoyed writing them. Stop by www.kdwrites.com for news of upcoming books.*

*kd easley*

# kd easley

# Nine Kinds of TROUBLE

NukeWorks
Publishing

NukeWorks Publishing
Fulton, Mo 65251 USA

ISBN 978-0-9825294-0-9

Front cover artwork  Gay Melody Sullivan

Cover design  A&J Creative Services.  www.aandjcreativeservices.com

Visit kd easley at www.kdwrites.com

Printed in U.S.A.

*For my mom, who was always my biggest fan.*
*I miss you.*

# Nine Kinds of TROUBLE

# Acknowledgements

Writing may be a solitary journey, but publishing, like child rearing, takes a village. So here's an attempt to thank the many that made this possible. First to Stacy Juba and Lisa Polisar, you've read my stuff when it was little more than a first draft and still you come back for more. Thanks for being there. Then, to A&J Creative Sercvices for keeping my website running, as well as my computer. To Gay Melody Sullivan for not throwing me out when I ask for a painting with a road tractor and a pregnancy test in it. The painting is perfect, thanks. To Alice Peck, editor extraordinaire and Chief of the Echo Police, I didn't subject her to these stories, but over the years, just working with her has made me a better writer. A huge thank you to my sons Justin and Clint who read the real first drafts, put up with an absentee mom, learned to cook and do the laundry so the house kept running when I was lost in my work and were always ready to 'read this for me' even when I interrupted their video games. And finally to my mother, who wasn't afraid to criticize even if she knew I'd get mad. She was always right and I always eventually saw things her way. Thanks, mom. You were supposed to be here for the book launch and fate intervened, I expect you to make your presence known.

# After Hours

A scream echoed off the walls of the quiet building. I jumped and glanced out my office door. The hallway was dark. The building was empty except for my boss, Larry, the shop foreman. It was his scream I'd heard. I walked slowly down the hall and peered into the darkened shop. The nightlights threw deep shadows around the hulking road tractors parked inside.

"Larry" I whispered. "You okay?"

There was no answer. I crept forward and kicked something soft. Stifling a yelp, I knelt beside the still form on the floor. It was Larry. His eyes stared unseeing at the ceiling; a bloody inch and a half combination wrench lay on the floor next to his head. Blood matted his hair and dribbled onto the floor.

A shuffling noise came from the far end of the shop then a crash followed by a curse. I scrambled to my feet and hid in the shadow of a Peterbuilt, eyes squeezed shut to make me invisible. The noises moved closer, boots scraping on concrete. I took a deep breath, opened my eyes and proceeded to make the dumbest move of my life.

"Anybody out there?" I called.

The shop went silent. I gave myself a mental head slap for entering the too stupid to live sweepstakes and slipped away from the truck and into the hallway. Footsteps sounded behind me getting louder. I scrambled down the hall and grabbed the door to the sales floor. It was locked. The steps turned into the hall and

1

squeaked on the polished floor. I swallowed a whimper and huddled in the shadow of the Coke machine. My pursuer stopped and changed direction. I let out a sigh of relief, ran silently into the parts room and pulled the door closed behind me. I was now surrounded on three sides by a chest high service counter and closed in by the door. I sagged with relief until the chirp of steps against the tile grew louder, then stopped outside my hiding place. I scrabbled gracelessly over the counter and cowered beneath. The door opened. I held my breath. A few endless seconds later the door closed softly. I strained to hear the sound of breathing over my pounding heart. I didn't hear anything; I hoped that meant I was alone.

Before I could talk myself out of it, I leaped to my feet and ran into the parts warehouse. No nightlights relieved the gloom back there; just darkness filled with the deeper shadows of shelves and hulking engine crates. I felt my way down the aisles and stopped. The footsteps sounded again, louder now, big, thumping, monstrous stomps echoing in the dark. I bit my lip to keep from sobbing and backed away from the noise.

"LuAnn! That you LuAnn? You should have gone home early tonight."

I knew that voice, Ace Miller, our lead mechanic. Why had he killed Larry? Why was he chasing me?

The soft nightlights shone through the windows of the front parts room putting me in silhouette. I ducked around a corner and backed amongst the belts and radiator hoses. They clattered softly beside my head as Ace moved closer.

"Come on out, LuAnn. I won't hurt you."

My stomach clenched in terror. I dove out of my protected hiding place and raced between the shelves. The thud of heavy booted feet pounding on concrete sounded behind me as I ran. I stopped at a rack of sheet aluminum used for repairing trailers. A small scrap was lying on top, three inches wide by maybe three feet long. I slid it off the shelf and backed against the wall as Ace ran toward me calling my name. When he got within range, I swung the aluminum scrap as hard as I could. It hit him in the neck. Ace crumpled to the floor and gurgled at my feet. Blood pooled darkly on the concrete. I dropped the metal and sank onto an oil box, my trembling hands pressed tight between my knees.

The warehouse lights flashed on as someone ran toward me. I looked up and my heart stopped. Larry was racing down the aisle.

"But...But...you're dead!"

"Nah, me and Ace were just having a little fun with ya. We know how you're scared of the dark and all."

His eyes dropped from me to Ace lying on the floor.

"Jesus, Lu. I think he's dead."

Ace lay in an expanding lake of blood, his sightless eyes staring at the ceiling above. I covered my mouth with my hands and slipped to the floor.

"What do we do now?" Larry whispered.

# Letters from Iraq

June 19th—Northern Iraq

Dear Bets,

Wish you were here. No, scratch that. I wish I was there. This is no place for you. The heat, the sand, not to mention getting shot at. I'll sleep tonight and dream of being home with you and if we're lucky, our dreams will mesh and for a few hours we'll be together.

Man, do I sound homesick. I'm sorry. I am, but that's not what's really got me down. Dallas is dead and I'm having a hard time with it. I found him this morning when we went out on patrol. It bothers me, the way he died. I went over the scene while I was waiting for the medics. I don't think he was stabbed by an enemy soldier. The knife in his chest was American and there wasn't a fight. Dallas wouldn't have let someone sneak up on him like that. He was one of the best. No one wants to hear my opinion. Over here, I'm not a big city cop, I'm just a soldier.

I'm sorry to unload all this on you, but, well, I just needed someone to talk to, babe and for me, it's always been you. I love you Betsy.

Sweet Dreams,
Andy


June 22nd—Chicago, Ill


Andy,

Oh, Baby. I'm so sorry about Dallas. Dammit, I hate being so far apart. There's nothing I can do except tell you I'm sorry. He was a nice guy. I'm glad I got to meet him before you shipped out. Now I'll worry double for you. I felt better some how, knowing he was with you. I know that was probably silly, but you know how I am.

I wish there was something I could do to help. Are you certain he was murdered? You know how you go off on a tangent sometimes. And Dallas was your friend. Don't let your grief blind you to what's really there. You know I love you, but, Andy, please be careful not to step on any toes. You're not in Chicago. Stay safe sweetheart.


I love you,
Betsy


June 24th—Chicago, Ill


Hi Darlin,

We had a service for Dallas today. I can't even begin to tell you what that was like. It's so hard. He was so full of, I don't know...energy, life. He felt like we were doing something great over here. I do, too, but it was different with Dallas. He made all the hardship seem okay.

Do you have all my old letters? I know I've talked about most of the guys in my unit at one time or another. I need more information. There's stuff going on over here that doesn't have anything to do with the war. I guess there always is. An Army camp is like a small city, lots of stuff going on under the surface.

I hope you understand what I need, babe. I can't get any more specific.

Love you,
Andy


July 1st—Chicago, Ill


Andy,

Sorry so long getting back to you. You're last letter just arrived. I hope I understood what you wanted. I guess you were worried about censors. I'm trying to read your mind.

Billy Mac is from Tucson. He's married with four kids. His wife is fed up with the service and he thinks he'll be divorced by the time he gets home. (Is this the kind of stuff you want?)

Morgan is a loner. Not close to anyone in the unit, but you said you'd trust him with your life.

Weasel, (you never told me his real name) is always getting out of doing the hard stuff. Always kissing up to the officers. Nobody likes him much and you hate being sent out on patrol with him. He's from Little Rock and lives with his mama.

Hotshot is a cowboy. Les Green I think is his name. He's from Montana and you told me he was going to get himself killed because he's always trying to be a hero (don't let him get you killed).

Hollywood is the surfer you brought over before you shipped out. He's gorgeous. (sorry, it's true) Seemed like a pretty nice kid to me. You haven't said much about him since you got there.

Wenton is an officer, (yours? I don't remember. After a while, the names run together. Sorry, I'm probably not helping much) You said he's arrogant and most of the guys in the unit don't care for him much. But, you also said he was a good soldier. I'm not sure I understand that. If the guys in his unit don't like him, how can he be a good soldier?

Those are all I can find. I'll look through the rest of the letters after work tonight. Andy, I'm worried about you. Don't get so wrapped up with Dallas that you forget to watch your back. What kind of stuff is going on over there? I can hardly sleep nights now worrying about you.

Please come home safe,
Betsy


July 4th—Northern Iraq


Happy Fourth of July, babe,

We're having the sandstorm to end all sandstorms here. It's starting to taper off, finally. Dammit, they're calling us out. I'll finish this later.

Continued July 6th

Hey darlin, just got back. One of our patrol units got lost in the storm. We found them. Hollywood was dead. Billy Mac and I were together when we found the body. He was shot in the back of the head. The big dicks are saying it was a sniper. Betsy, that's bullshit. A sniper's not going to be out in a sandstorm. Hollywood and Dallas were running-mates. He and I have been hanging out a lot since Dallas died. He thinks, well thought, Dallas was murdered, too. And now he's dead. I think the Iraqi's are the least of my worries over here.

I need you to do another favor, babe. The stuff you found was good.

Hollywood's patrol unit was Wenton, Weasel and Morgan. Steven Wenton, from Madison, WI, Donny Ray Moore, Little Rock and Denzel Morgan, Denver, I think. I'll try to find out more. Can you talk to Sgt. Linden down at the station house? I'm afraid, Betsy. Really afraid, and not of the enemy.

Gotta go,
Andy


July 10th—Chicago, Ill


Hi Andy,

Spent Fourth of July with your Mom and Dad out on the lake. It wasn't the same without you here. I'm so afraid. I wish you could get out of that unit.

I talked to Sgt. Linden for you. He pulled some information. I think I know now what kind of thing is going on under the surface. My hands are trembling as I write this letter. Andy, you have to be careful. These guys are serous. Talk to Morgan and keep close to him and Billy Mac. Keep your eyes open and for God's sake, don't let anyone but those two know you think Hollywood and Dallas were murdered.

Stay safe,
Bets


July 20th—Chicago, Ill


Andy,

It's been so long since I've heard from you. I know you could be out on patrol or something. I know it's hot over there right now. I'm watching the news every night praying not to hear your unit is involved. This is horrible, waiting, not knowing. It was bad enough that you were in a war zone, now with this other. I want you home so bad it hurts.

Sgt. Linden came over today. I've gotten to the point I don't even want to talk to him. I have information that you need and no way to get it to you. This is the best I can do. The two W's are not on your side. They've got friends higher up, that's why there hasn't been a murder investigation. Is there an officer there you can trust? Andy, be careful. Just drop the investigation and come home safe.

I love you,
Betsy


July 31st—Chicago, Ill


Andy, I can't stand this not knowing. It's been weeks. I hope you've gotten my letters. I pray every night that you are safe. I live in fear that I'm going to get a knock on the door telling me you're…I can't even say it. I want you home so bad. Drop this investigation, Andy. They will kill you. I need you here. Please remember you aren't in Chicago. Please, Andy, for me.

Betsy


August 9th—Northern Iraq


Hi darlin,

I've been out of touch, and I know it's been hard on you. Hang on and trust me. It's gonna be okay. I got your letters. Got one from Linden, too. This is all going to be over soon. Billy Mac is on his way home. He was wounded when our caravan was attacked. We were so careful, but they knew our route, they knew our plans. I sent my information out with him. Linden is going to meet him and get the information to

10

someone that can help. I just don't know who I can trust over here except for Morgan. He and I are together 24/7. It's the only way we can stay safe. I hope you've saved all my letters. Someone from Intelligence will probably contact you and take them. Make copies if you want to keep them. I'm sure they won't give them back. This is bigger than you can imagine. I wish I could tell you more. Just hang on and trust me.

I love you,
Andy


August 15th—Chicago, Ill


Andy,

I got your letter today. A day late. Some officer from Army Intelligence came in yesterday and took all your letters. They searched the whole apartment and wouldn't tell me anything. Andy, what's going on. I'm so afraid.

Betsy


September 1st—Saudi Arabia


Hey darlin,

It's almost over, I promise. Wenton and Weasel are gone along with General Batts and Colonel Stephens. They were selling information to the Iraqis. Dallas and Hollywood found out, but they took their information to the wrong officer. They died along with I don't know how many other young men. It makes me sick that the General could corrupt those good men.

Wenton and Stephens were fine soldiers, but the General found a way to get to them.

There is some good news. We're off of the front lines now and hope to head to Germany soon. Morgan and I are going to be stuck with the intelligence guys for a while, so I'll be out of touch. Hang on just a little longer. Without your help, I couldn't have pulled this off.

Linden said Billy Mac is doing well and his wife seems happy to see him again. There's one happy ending in the god-awful mess. The next one will be when I hold you in my arms.

I love you, Betsy, can't wait to get home to Chicago.
Andy

# Nothing Much Has Changed

We're done here, Randi, let's call it a day."

The look of relief that crossed my face made Granny Bert laugh. She walked out the door of Mabel's café looking as fresh as when she went in that morning. I stumbled out behind her. My hair was plastered in wet curls against my face and down my neck. My legs felt like rubber, my back felt broken. I groaned and sagged against the outside wall of the diner.

"I don't know how you do it, Granny."

Granny Bert, my dad's mom, is eighty years old. She's waited tables at Mabel's from five in the morning until two in the afternoon, six days a week, since Mabel opened in 1957. After work, she putters around in her garden or goes shopping. Today she voted for shopping. I was trying to figure out how to get out of it.

I was thirty-nine, I'd just put in four hours of waiting tables to cover for Mabel's annual trip to the dentist. I had forty-nine dollars worth of pity tips stuffed in the left front pocket of my Levi's and I couldn't have felt any worse if I'd just finished running a marathon.

I peeled myself off the wall and trudged down the street behind Granny Bert. My truck was sitting under a big oak tree. Unfortunately the shade was on the other side of the tree. Heat waves shimmered off the roof. I sighed. It was going to be sweltering inside and my AC didn't work. My fondest wish was to make it home to the shower before I ran into anyone I knew. If my life ran true to form, my wish most likely wouldn't come true.

I moved up beside Granny Bert to ask if she wanted to eat dinner with me and my boys. She interrupted before I could speak.

"What's that guy doing to your truck?"

I glanced up and stared down the street. A man had a coat hanger stuck through the window and was trying to unlock my door.

"Hey," I yelled. "Hey, you. Get away from my truck."

He glanced up in surprise and redoubled his efforts. Granny took off toward him at a dead run.

"Granny, stop. What are you doing?"

Exasperated, I coaxed my legs into moving and tried to catch her. The man said something I couldn't hear as Granny drew close to him. She stopped and swung her industrial sized purse at his head. Lucky for him, he ducked. The weight of the bag turned Granny around and before she caught her balance, the stranger swung open the door and pushed her inside. I put on a burst of speed, but before I could catch them, he was backing out of the parking space. I planted a foot on the rear bumper and tumbled myself over the tailgate as the truck squealed off down the street.

I lay in the bed of the truck squashed up against the toolbox. The metal floor felt like it was burning stripes through my shirt. Afraid to sit up, I swore and huddled out of sight of the rear view mirror. The truck sped through downtown while I tried to figure out what to do next. Something hard and lumpy pressed hard into my back. I slithered to the side and pulled it out from under a tarp. My eyes widened in surprise. It was my brother Chad's 9mm Glock with no magazine. I laughed. I remembered him slipping it under the tarp last night when he got conned into playing catch with my boys. He was probably going nuts trying to figure out where it was.

I lay back on the musty canvas and tried to figure out how my brother's unloaded gun was going to help. The truck made a screeching left turn and I slid across the bed, feet first. Something hard skittered across the rough surface and whacked into my head.

"Ouch."

I reached up to grab the offending trash and found Chad's spare radio. We made a hard right hand turn and before I could grab onto anything I slid head first into the other side of the bed. My eyes teared up and I swore.

I eased up onto my knees and peeked over the toolbox. Granny Bert's mouth was moving, but I couldn't hear anything over the wind noise. She was having the desired effect on our kidnapper, though. He was holding her off with one hand and trying to drive with the other. His attention was totally focused on what was in the cab with him and what the truck was heading toward. I was pretty certain that if I ripped off my clothes and stood up in the bed, he wouldn't notice. I gave Granny a mental thumbs up and sunk down behind the box to use the radio. My luck, it probably wasn't charged.

I turned the knob on the police radio and it lit up. I gave a silent thank you to the god of electronics and keyed the mic.

"Dispatch," I whispered. "My grandmother and I have been carjacked." I leaned up and peered around to get my bearings. "We're on Timber Bridge Road, almost to the turn-off at the campground."

I let up on the button and waited. If the dispatcher was surprised at a non-police voice crackling through on a department frequency, she didn't show it. Oozing calm, she came on and asked me to repeat. I did. She assured me help was on the way and I dropped the radio in relief. Now all I had to do was wait.

The wind swirled around the bed of the truck as we raced down Timber Bridge Road, turning my wet curls into a tangled rat's nest. I pushed the hair out of my eyes and stared out the back of the truck for any sign of help. The road behind us remained empty. I groaned in frustration and thunked my head back against the toolbox. Where were the cops? Where were my brothers? Dammit, what good was it having family on the police force if they weren't around to rescue me when I needed it.

The campground turn-off flashed by on my left and the truck slid into a hard right turn. I fell over and slid headfirst into the truck bed. This guy was really starting to tick me off. I sat up, keyed the mic to let dispatch know where we were when the truck slid off the road and stopped abruptly against a tree. My head smacked hard against the metal toolbox, the radio flew from my

15

grasp and clattered across the truck bed. My eyes filled with tears of pain.

The engine shut off. I could hear it ticking in the silence of the woods. Then Granny Bert yelled. I heard the sound of a blow, then the driver's door popped open. I flattened myself against the floor of the bed and prayed our maniac didn't look back. He didn't, he had other things on his mind. Thinking he was alone, he walked away from the truck and slid down the zipper on his khakis. While he was watering the road ditch, I leaned up for a look in the cab. Granny Bert was lying on the seat, a red patch on her cheek where the guy had punched her.

Anger surged through my body. I grabbed the empty gun, slipped over the side of the truck and stuck it in the stranger's back, kidney high. His stream came to an abrupt halt.

"Put your hands in the air."

He paused in confusion, my gun in his back, his hands cradling his Johnson. I pressed the gun hard against his shirt.

"Now!" I yelled.

His hands came up. His flow restarted and his nice clean khakis got a big wet patch down the front.

"Don't shoot," he whispered.

"You killed my Granny."

"No. No. She's not dead. I promise."

"She better not be."

Sirens sounded in the distance. I let out my breath in relief. My captive, feeling me relax, jerked away and started to run. Well hobble. His gate was somewhat impaired by the fact that he was still hanging out of his fly.

As a police car slid to a stop behind the truck, I took out after the carjacker. He turned around once to see how close I was. The view of his thing flopping around outside his pants was a visual I could have done without. He turned back around, tripped and stumbled. I made a flying leap and hoped I hit the his backside, not his front. I was already as acquainted with that as I wanted to be.

I hit him just above the hips and we tumbled down a small drainage ditch in a tangle of body parts that I really didn't want to think about. I felt the brush of wet fabric against my skin and shuddered. Eeeuw.

When we landed at the bottom, I realized Chad's gun was still clenched in my fist. I smacked him above the left ear and jabbed it into his temple. He went still. Footsteps crashed through the brush behind us.

"Police, drop the weapon."

I dropped the gun and raised my hands. Someone pulled me away from the carjacker and deposited me unceremoniously to the side. I stumbled, fell, righted myself and leaned against a tree. My legs were shaking and my knees didn't want to keep me upright.

The officers, one in uniform that I recognized and one in plainclothes that I didn't, read him his rights and snapped on the handcuffs. They jerked him off the ground and laughed when they saw him flopping outside his pants. The uniform officer pushed him forward toward the parked cruiser.

The plainclothes detective turned toward me and my heart stopped. My knees, almost steady, went weak again and I grabbed the tree for support. AJ Weleski, the man that had broken my heart nearly twenty years before, stared across the small clearing.

"Randi Jennings," he whispered.

I'm glad he said my name, I'd forgotten it.

"Black. It's Randi Black, now," I said.

His face went rigid. "Right, I'd forgotten about that."

I swallowed a smile. AJ and my ex husband, Morgan Black, were legendary enemies in high school. Didn't look like twenty years had changed AJ's opinion any.

I took in the figure in front of me as he eyed my tattered form. AJ was still as gorgeous as the day he'd left for the Army. The effect those almost black eyes had on me hadn't changed much, either. I swallowed once and tried to remember to breathe. I glanced down at my grass and mud stained clothes, reached one hand up to my rat's nest hair and sighed. I looked like a nightmare. I glanced back at AJ and got that lazy grin that made women want to fling their clothes off and lay down at his feet. Granny Bert burst through the trees and the spell was broken.

"Where is he," she yelled. "Where is that low down piece of dog turd?"

"Well hi, Miss Bertie," AJ said.

Granny stopped in her tracks.

"AJ Weleski. When did you get back into town?"

He walked forward to take her arm and leaned close to speak. She smiled and blushed. They moved through the trees toward my truck. I trudged along behind. Man, AJ's back view hadn't lost anything in the last twenty years. It may have even improved.

AJ turned and glanced at me over his shoulder. Caught looking, I blushed. He winked and that slow smile spread across his lips.

"Doesn't look like much has changed around here," he said.

I felt that old familiar tingle deep inside and ducked my head. Nope, nothing much had changed.

Watch for Randi, Granny, and AJ in the upcoming novel Timber Bridge. Coming 2010 from NukeWorks Publishing — Keep checking www.kdwrites.com for updates.

# Sting

*H*i, I'm Sgt. Dean Michaels and I'd like to welcome you to the twenty-fourth annual Citizens Police Academy."

Mandy slithered lower in her chair. She really regretted starting this class. The fear that had inspired it was already starting to fade. Sgt. Michaels introduced the Chief and stepped aside as he said a few words. Mandy tuned out. She stifled a sigh and glanced around the room. Her eyes stopped on a tall dark haired man slouched against the coffee pot. He was in a white shirt, dark blue utilities and a navy blue jacket. Around the upper arms of the coat, stripes of reflective tape glittered under the florescent lights. He caught her glance and smiled. His teeth flashed white against his tan. Mandy's heart took an involuntary leap. She looked quickly toward the front of the room where the Chief was finishing his welcome speech. A small smile curved her lips. Maybe this class wouldn't be so bad after all.

Sgt. Michaels introduced the rest of the instructors, then turned the podium over to Officer Mark Jefferson. The tall dark police officer peeled himself off the wall and stepped to the front of the classroom. His eyes locked with Mandy's as he started to speak. At the coffee pot during break, Mandy looked up to find the handsome officer at her side. She introduced herself and asked about doing a ride-along. Jefferson grinned.

"How bout we do it tonight? You can ride with me. I'll set it up."

Mandy agreed and joined him after class. They drove through the dark city, silent except for the chatter of the police radio. Jefferson broke the silence.

"Why'd you take the CPA class? You interested in law enforcement?"

"Not really, it just seemed like it might be fun."

The real reason was a guy called Shark. The CPA offered two voluntary classes in self-defense. Mandy wanted those classes. She was afraid of Shark.

"Well, has it been fun so far?"

Mandy grinned. "It's getting better."

Jefferson smiled and pulled into a parking lot off Madison. He pointed the radar gun down the hill and they waited. The street stayed empty. The silence in the car grew strained.

"Your job always this boring?" Mandy finally asked.

Jefferson laughed. "Sometimes boring, sometimes more excitement than you can imagine."

Mandy yawned. "I wouldn't mind a little excitement right now."

As if on cue, the police radio crackled to life. Jefferson had the car rocketing down the hill before Mandy had even deciphered the message. The siren split the quiet night. She locked her fingers on the door handle and tried to stay in her seat as they raced across town. They slid around a corner and Mandy's head smacked the window.

"You might want to put on your seatbelt," Jefferson said.

Mandy rubbed the sore spot on her head. "What's going on?"

She glanced at the speedometer as the needle crept toward one hundred.

"That was Stevens, he's in trouble."

They squealed around another corner and Jefferson slid the car to a stop. "You stay here."

He launched out the door of the car and ran toward the building. A group of people clustered around a figure on the ground outside. Jefferson paused at the group, slipped his gun from the holster and ran down the street. He disappeared around the corner of the building into the darkness. Mandy leaned forward trying to see what was going on.

More police cars slid to a stop around them, more officers joined the group. An ambulance pulled in followed by a fire truck. The building glowed in the eerie flash of emergency lights. More people poured from surrounding doorways and gathered on the lawns.

The radio crackled, officers peeled away from the group and raced toward the dark corner where Jefferson had disappeared. Mandy, curiosity overriding common sense, slipped out of the cruiser and made her way to the still figure on the sidewalk.

The crowd parted as she approached and the figure on the ground became visible. Mandy gasped and took an involuntary step back. Luther Wallace lay on the ground, shirt front blood soaked, eyes staring blankly at the sky.

Mandy sank to her knees. An ambulance crew ran past with a gurney. She stared at the body on the ground in front of her and shuddered. The ambulance crew returned with a uniformed officer buckled to the gurney. They shoved it into the back of the truck and squealed away.

A hand roughly grasped her shoulder and jerked her to her feet. She shrieked in surprise.

"What the hell are you doing out of the car."

Mandy, eyes wide, swallowed once and stared into the angry face of Mark Jefferson.

"God dammit, I told you to stay in the car."

Mandy pointed a shaky finger at the body on the ground. "I know him," she whispered.

Jefferson pushed her to the car and shoved her roughly inside. He slid behind the wheel and stared at Mandy.

"What do you know about the victim?"

"I...he's...um." Mandy took a deep breath and started again. "I used to date him. His name's Luther Wallace. We, um...split up a couple of months ago. I didn't like some of the people he hung out with so I broke it off."

Jefferson pulled away from the curb and drove across town toward the hospital. Mandy sat quietly beside him waiting for him to speak. When it was clear he wasn't going to, she broke the silence.

"That officer, is he. Was he shot?"

Jefferson grunted a yes.

"Is he going to be okay?"

He greeted her question with silence. Mandy scooted toward the door and tried to shrink into the upholstery.

"Luther didn't shoot that cop," she said.

It was a statement that sounded like a question. Jefferson picked up the inflection and stared at her as he pulled into the parking lot of St. Anthony's Hospital.

"What makes you think that?"

"He wouldn't do that."

"Hmph. How long'd you date that asshole?"

Mandy didn't answer, just stared out the window.

"Come on Mandy. What makes you so sure he couldn't shoot a cop?"

"He didn't have a gun."

Jefferson laughed.

Mandy glared at him. "If he had a gun, I would have known it."

"Look, Mandy. Luther was what we call a frequent flyer around here. Every officer knows him. Most of us have busted him. He's been run in on gun charges, drugs, burglary, domestic violence and just about everything else you can think of. How the hell did you ever get hooked up with him?"

"He worked for my dad."

"Luther Wallace was an asshole."

Mandy stared down at her hands. They were clasped in her lap to hide the shaking. She didn't want Jefferson to see how upset she was. Luther was dead. All the self-defense classes in the world weren't going to help her now.

"I don't think Luther shot Stevens." Mandy looked up as she spoke.

"We'll know for sure after they retrieve the bullets. But in my gut, I don't think it was Luther either," he replied.

Jefferson didn't know it, but that made Mandy feel worse. If Luther had gone off half cocked and shot a cop before getting himself killed, her troubles would be over. Unfortunately, she agreed with Jefferson. Luther didn't shoot that cop.

Mandy followed Jefferson into the ER waiting room at St. Anthony's. Captain Martinez glared at her when she came through the door.

"Jefferson, what the hell are you doing here with your ride-along?"

Jefferson looked at Mandy in surprise.

"I'm sorry sir. I'll get her back to the station right away. Have you heard anything about Stevens?"

"He's in surgery."

Jefferson spun Mandy around and guided her through the doors. They got into the cruiser without speaking. As they approached the station parking lot, he broke the silence.

"Will you be home in the morning? I want to find out what else you know about Luther."

She nodded. He parked and waited for Mandy to exit. She paused with her hand on the door.

"He was afraid of a guy they called Shark."

Jefferson's head came up in surprise. He nodded once and scribbled something in his notebook.

"I'll contact you tomorrow."

He fished a card out of his pocket and handed it to her. Mandy shivered as their fingers brushed. She saw the touch hadn't gone unnoticed by Jefferson either. He pulled his hand back and stared through the windshield.

"If you think of something that I need to know before then, my pager number's on the card."

"Thanks. I'm sorry I got in the way tonight."

Jefferson looked up and smiled, his teeth a white flash in the darkness.

"Look, don't worry about it. I shouldn't have come down on you like that."

"It's okay. I understand."

Mandy stepped out of the cruiser and trudged through the parking lot to her car. Footsteps scuffed behind her. She sped up. When she reached her car, she jabbed the keys toward the door lock just as a hand clamped around her arm. She stifled a scream. Shark, collar up, hat pulled low, leaned close and whispered in her ear.

"I noticed you at the crime scene tonight. You came in with that cop Jefferson. You got somethin goin with a cop now? Hmm?"

"I'm not dating a cop."

"Luther went to the cops. Now he's dead. That stupid kid Stevens is probably a goner too. You know what's good for ya, you'll stay away from the fuckin cops."

Mandy swallowed and jerked her arm out of Shark's grasp. He laughed and shambled off into the night. Mandy scooted behind the wheel of her car and waited for the shaking to subside.

\* \* \*

Mandy lay in the dark listening to the sounds of the house. At every creak or groan she jumped. Finally she gave up on sleep and went to the living room. In the darkness she thought about Luther. If he'd just kept his mouth shut and stayed out of trouble for one more week, everything would have been fine. God, she should have picked a partner with an IQ over 40.

Shark was a problem too. There was no way he should have figured out what was going on already. Just one more week and they would have been home free. Mandy sighed in frustration. She just needed a few more days to set up the sale. Then she was out of this two-bit town forever. She smiled to herself. This could still work out okay. With Luther gone, all the money would be hers. She just needed to play Officer Jefferson along for a few days. Keep his attention focused on something other than police work. She remembered the tingle when their fingers touched and smiled again. She didn't think that was going to be a problem. She strolled through the darkened living room and slipped back into bed.

She answered the knock at her door the next morning in the shorts and tee shirt she'd worn to bed. Her eyes were heavy lidded with sleep and her hair artfully tousled from the pillows. It was all an act. She'd been up for hours.

Officer Jefferson stood on her doorstep. "Sorry, did I get you out of bed?"

She smiled and ran her had through her tangled hair. "Don't worry about it. I needed to get up anyway."

He followed her into the house.

"Can I get you a cup of coffee?" she asked.

He shook his head.

"Have a seat. I've got to have a cup. I'll be right back."

She poured a cup of coffee, combed the tangles out of her hair and slipped into skintight jeans and a tank top. Jefferson was perched on the edge of a chair in the living room when she came back in.

His eyes gave her a quick once over before he slipped back into cop mode. Mandy smiled to herself and sat down across from him.

"Sorry to bother you, but I need to talk to you about Luther," he said.

She put the coffee cup on the table and leaned forward as he spoke. His eyes dropped from her face to her chest. Mandy bit her lip to hide the smile.

They went over her relationship with Luther from the beginning. She told him they'd dated for a few weeks, then she dumped him. She didn't know about his criminal background. She fought back tears and apologized because she couldn't really tell him much more.

Jefferson handed her a tissue from the box on the table. She sniffed and wiped her eyes.

"Sorry, I don't usually do this. It's just. I didn't get much sleep last night."

"Hey, I understand." He gave her arm a reassuring squeeze and again she felt the tingle pass between them.

Jefferson stood quickly and thanked her for her time. Mandy followed him to the door.

"How is Officer Stevens? Is he going to be okay?" she asked.

"He didn't make it," he said quietly.

"Oh. I'm sorry."

* * *

At the next CPA class, Officer Jefferson did a short session on drugs. Mandy cringed inside and tried to look interested. Her buy was finally set up. She would meet the guy at the Road House tomorrow night at nine. At Nine-thirty she intended to be out of town, thirty-thousand dollars richer than she was right now.

Thirty thousand of Shark's dollars safe in her pocket and not a backward glance for this rat-hole town.

Officer Jefferson had been a bit of a problem. He kept stopping by and asking dangerous questions, but she was sure he didn't suspect her. He was more interested in other things. A couple of late-night visits from Shark hadn't helped her nerves much either. All in all, she was going to be glad when tomorrow was over.

During break, she and Officer Jefferson again met at the coffee pot.

"Hey there," he said. "After last week, I wasn't sure you'd show up again."

"I'm not a quitter."

He smiled and brushed her arm. "Glad to hear that. What ya doin after class?"

Mandy smiled.

"What'd ya have in mind?" she asked.

"Late dinner, maybe?"

"Sounds good."

Class started again and Mandy doodled in her workbook while a lady from records droned on about how the paperwork was handled. When the class was over, she shot out the door. Officer Jefferson was outside in civvies waiting for her.

He walked her to her car, then they went out for dinner. After the second beer, Mandy was pretty sure where they'd finish the night. When they parked outside her house. She made sure of it.

"Wanna come in for a drink?" she asked.

Jefferson smiled and followed Mandy into the house. A couple of drinks and some soft music and pretty soon things were going just the way she wanted. Or she thought so until she invited him to stay the night. His lips said no, but the look in his eyes said something else. She slipped her arms around his neck, kissed him softly on the lips and asked again. She could feel his response to her body and was sure of his answer this time.

"Sorry, Mandy. I better get home."

She dropped her arms in frustration and stepped back.

"Well, aren't you the officer and the gentleman," she snapped.

He cupped her cheek in his hand and brushed his thumb across her lips.

"Maybe some other time."

In disbelief, she watched as his car pulled out of her drive and disappeared into the night.

* * *

The Road House was dark and filled with cigarette smoke. Mandy couldn't wait to get out of there. She had plans for that thirty thousand and they didn't include sitting around in this sleazy bar.

At one minute after nine, her buyer slid into the booth across from her. They chatted for a minute then he left to get a drink. On the seat where he'd been sitting was an envelope. She picked it up and in its place left a small package wrapped in brown paper. She smiled in satisfaction when he came back with their drinks.

"Pleasure doing business with you," she toasted him with her beer.

He smiled and clinked bottles before he drank. Dancing with impatience, she forced herself to finish the beer before she got up to leave. She nodded once to her buyer and pushed her way through the crowd to the door. As she stepped outside, a dark form peeled out of the shadows and grabbed her arm. She yelped in surprise.

"Mark," she stammered as Officer Jefferson stepped into the light.

"You're under arrest," he said.

"What are you talking about? I just came in here for a beer."

Jefferson snapped on the handcuffs and started reading her rights.

"What are you doing? Mark, what's going on?"

A second form slipped out of the shadows. Shark.

Mandy jerked back and the handcuffs pinched on her trapped wrists.

"Ow. Wait. What's he doing here? What's going on?"

"You got things under control here, Jefferson?" Shark asked.

"Yeah, we're good to go. Thanks, man."

Shark nodded and pushed through the door into the bar. Mandy stared at Officer Jefferson in confusion.

"He's a cop?"

Jefferson smiled and pushed her across the parking lot toward his cruiser. "Uh huh."

Mandy sighed. "And the guy in the bar?" Was he a cop too?"

"Yup."

"Shit. No wonder you didn't spend the night at my house."

Jefferson laughed softly. "It was tempting."

Mandy was silent as they made their way to the police station. As they pulled up outside something that had been bothering her registered.

"Jefferson. Who shot Officer Stevens?"

"Stevens didn't get shot."

"Well, then who shot Luther?"

Jefferson's movie star grin flashed at her from the mirror.

"Nobody."

"You mean I was set up from the beginning?"

He turned and grinned at her over his shoulder.

"Yup. When we picked up Luther, he couldn't start talking fast enough."

"I should never have taken that stupid police academy class," Mandy muttered under her breath as he led her into the station.

"We'd a just got you some other way," Jefferson said with a smile.

# Vanity's Price

*T*he face peering from the mirror was unlined, the skin as smooth and soft as a woman half her age. Despite a pack-a-day habit and an infrequent beauty regimen, she remained flawless. Maria stepped away from the mirror and gazed at her full reflection. The body suffered a bit of middle aged spread, but she'd stack it up against almost anyone. She grinned at the pun and cupped her full breasts with her hands. Perky but not aggressive, she thought. Not like those bionic knockers in Hollywood.

She stepped back to the mirror, applied a light coating of makeup and slipped into her clothes. Back to the mirror again, she fought with her hopelessly thinning hair and sighed.

In frustration the tossed the hairbrush at the wall and watched silently as it rebounded into the toilet.

"Fine, I don't need it anyway. Who needs a hairbrush when they don't have hair?"

As she strode out of the house, she was no longer the slim, confident woman that had cupped her breasts and assessed her face critically in the mirror. She was a sad, slumping, forty-year old woman with thinning hair.

As she wove through traffic on her way to work, she tried to come up with a plausible excuse to stay home, but nothing came and too soon, she was settled at her desk for another long, boring day.

Gone were the times when guys would shuffle behind her chair and playfully tug her ponytail. Gone were the days when she would catch the appreciative eye of a client as he made his way through the office and it was all because of her hair. The body was the same, the face was the same. Just the hair was different.

"Dammit, it's just not fair."

A head popped over the cubicle divider, Andy, the office gossip.

"What's a matter, love?"

Maria glanced at Andy and realized she must have spoken out loud.

"Nothing, just this damn computer. It's working now."

Andy looked disappointed.

"That's too bad, I was hoping you had some juicy new gossip or maybe a little teaser about your love life."

"Hmph. Not likely."

Andy dropped back behind his cubicle and Maria stared at her screen in disgust. She logged onto the internet and searched for sites that dealt with female hair loss. They were few and far between. Mostly there were cranks selling miracle drugs, wigmakers, people touting amazing results from vitamins. Finally, a tiny add caught her eye.

"Permanent solution to hair loss. Works for men and women. Call today for a free appointment."

Maria jotted the number and closed her browser window as her boss, Chase, walked through the door. She followed him with her eyes enjoying the view and sighed again. Forget it Mar, he likes women with hair.

When he was safely past, she picked up the phone and dialed. The Hair-Append system would see her after work. She hung up the phone and took a shuddering breath. This was it. This was all she needed to get that promotion and attract a man. Maybe even Chase.

The rest of the afternoon she dreamed of walking the beach with the wind whispering through her hair and no longer having to worry about her blinding scalp showing through. Time crawled by, but finally she was free to change her life.

She raced across town and took the elevator to an unmarked office on the fifth floor. Soft music flooded the room and everyone waiting was smiling. She gave her name at the window and took a seat. She picked up a magazine and from behind its pages, she studied the others waiting for their appointments. Their hair looked natural and there wasn't a bald head to be seen anywhere. They called her name and on trembling legs she walked into the stylist's cubicle.

They discussed the system, how it worked, what was expected of the clients and the cost. Before they finished explaining it, Maria was writing a check. They leaned her back into the chair, shaved what little hair she had and coated her head with polymers. After a short wait, the new hair was fitted into place. While she waited for the polymers to set, she read all their information on the hair. It would last for three to five years, the polymers had to be redone every three months but between times, if she used the correct hair care products, there would be no problems. They'd never had a dissatisfied customer, she was assured.

She read testimonials and talked to customers that were there to get their polymers rejuvenated. They were thrilled with their new look and assured her she would be a new woman. Confident, beautiful and she'd never have to do the old comb-over again.

She poured through style books and finally settled on a hairstyle that was perfect. As promised, Maria left Hair-Append a new woman.

She drove to the mall, purchased a clingy new outfit and a pair of sexy shoes. She ran home, retouched her makeup, slipped into the slinky new dress and went to town to try out her new hair.

A bounce in her step and a twinkle in her eyes, she swayed into the Paradise Club and slipped onto a barstool. Before she could even sip her drink, an incredible looking man sat down beside her.

"Maria?"

She glanced over. It was her boss.

"Chase, hi."

"Let me buy you a drink," he said. "Come join us at our table."

Maria picked up her drink and followed Chase across the room.

"You must have done something different with your hair," he said. "It looks fantastic."

Maria murmured her thanks and felt that the ten-thousand dollars she'd spent that afternoon had already paid off. Chase's glance took in the form fitting dress, the let's get it on shoes and rested his hand briefly on her hip.

"The rest of the package is not too bad either," he whispered as he pulled out her chair.

Maria woke the next morning on plum colored satin sheets and felt the pull of seldom used muscles and she stretched. Her smile was permanently fixed. Chase walked into the room with a glass of orange juice and slid onto the bed next to her.

She leaned back against the pillows and took a sip.

"Why haven't I ever noticed how incredibly beautiful you are," he asked.

Maria smiled at her secret.

"Well, I don't dress the same at work. I guess that's it."

Chase ran his hands gently across her stomach and lightly kissed her breast.

"That's probably a good thing."


Maria's life continued on an upward spiral. It didn't take long for office gossip to tip to the fact that she was sleeping with the boss. But when their engagement was announced, mouths dropped open in surprise.

Maria was happier than she'd ever been, but there was something wrong with her hair. She went back for a check-up. They removed it, rejuvenated the polymers, reinstalled it and told her everything was fine, but Maria knew something was wrong. Her head felt funny. The hair didn't fit right. Even Chase mentioned it.

The morning of the wedding, Maria woke with a pounding headache. Her eyes were puffy and her head looked misshapen. In a panic, she called Hair-Append. They rushed her in, removed the hair. Once again, the polymers were rejuvenated and the hair was replaced, but it looked like a Halloween wig stuffed over a full head of hair. Maria was in a panic. She was only hours away from her wedding and her head was covered with lumps, her eyes were puffed and purple and her head was still pounding.

The hair technician assured her the hair was fine and she probably just had a virus. Maria demanded to see the manager, Mr. Lee. After a long consultation and a liberal dose of vodka, Maria's headache subsided and she left to prepare for the ceremony.

It was dreadful. She could hear people whispering about her head. When she turned to look, they averted their eyes.

My, God, she thought. What have I done in the name of vanity?

Just moments before the ceremony was to begin, her headache came back with a vengeance. She decided there was nothing to do, but tell Chase what was going on.

They sat in the bride's dressing room as Maria explained to Chase about the hair.

"You mean, underneath that, you're completely bald?" he said.

Maria nodded and tears washed down her face.

"Were you not going to tell me about this?"

Maria took a shuddering breath and tried to explain, but Chase was livid.

"What else haven't you told me? Any other sordid secrets in your past?"

Maria sobbed into her hands as Chase stormed out of the room. Hours later, the church silent and empty, Maria trudged through the door and drove to her apartment. Her head was lumpy, the newly rejuvenated polymers weren't holding. In anger she grabbed the hair and jerked. The hair popped free and Maria saw what was underneath for the first time. Lumps of flesh dotted her head. She touched them and they felt cold and slick like scar tissue. She stared at the lifeless hair in her hand and let it slide from her fingers.

Chase was gone. Her hair was gone. Her job was gone. Her life was over because of some stupid hair.

With steely resolve, she dug through the trunk her mother once bought for her to keep her trousseau. Inside, underneath the unused linens and newspaper wrapped crystal was a .22 Ruger target pistol, a gift from her father when she moved away from home.

She slid it into the waistband of her jeans and walked slowly around the apartment.

"The punishment should fit the crime," she muttered.

In the kitchen, under the sink, she looked through her household chemicals. Nothing there really suited her plans so she went to look in the garage. Next to the door was a bottle of charcoal lighter fluid. She smiled and took it into the house.

She gathered together her hair care products. She emptied one bottle, filled it three fourths of the way with shampoo. She topped it off with the lighter fluid and shook the bottle until they mixed. The shampoo had an odd greenish tinge but the fragrance covered up the smell of the lighter fluid.

She squirted a small amount into the sink, dropped in a match and watched as it whooshed into flame. Satisfied, she filled a second bottle and dropped it into her purse.

With the gun still tucked into her waistband and one bottle clutched in her hand, she stalked out the door and made her second trip to Hair-Append.

She pushed into the waiting room. Her lumpy, misshapen head gleamed in the lights without its normal covering of hair. Maria never noticed. She asked politely to speak with Mr. Lee and forced her way into his office before he could say no. Maria sat down in front of his desk and instructed him to send everyone home for the day. When he declined, she slipped the .22 out of her waistband and asked again. He sent everyone home.

Io While they waited for the office to clear, Maria got up and poured them each a drink. She was smiling, calm, sociable. Mr. Lee started to relax. When the office was empty except for them, Maria told him to follow her. She pushed him into the stylists chair and told him how he'd ruined her life.

She picked up the clippers and moved as if to shave his head. His eyes went wide. He wasn't a customer, his hair was real. He didn't want rejuvenated polymers on his head.

Maria put down the clippers and made him touch the nodules of flesh covering her head. He shrank away in disgust.

"Touch them!" she shouted.

Gingerly he reached out and brushed his fingers across her head.

"You need to pay for what you've done to me."

He sat up in the chair and gave her his best used car salesmen smile.

"I'll be more than happy to refund all your money," he said.

Maria smiled and followed him back to the office. He wrote a check and pressed it into her hand. Maria thanked him and motioned him back to the stylist's cubicle.

"That's a start," she said. "But you've not only ruined my head, you've ruined my life. Today was my wedding day. I got left at the alter. Forty-year-old women don't get second chances. Especially when they've got lumps all over their bald head."

Mr. Lee was speechless. The used car salesman smile was gone.

Maria pushed him back in the chair and turned on the water. His eyes got wide.

"Relax, I'm just going to wash your hair. Look," she said holding up the bottle. "I'm even using genuine Hair-Append products."

He swallowed and leaned back in the chair. Maria washed his hair then soaped it up again with an extra generous amount of shampoo. She told him to stay still then she reached into her bag for her cigarettes.

The shampoo, lighter fluid combination started burning his skin. The fumes made his eyes water. She lit her cigarette with a gold Zippo lighter and leaned toward his head with the open flame. The soap suds lit with a whoosh. The manager screamed and tried to get out of the chair. Before he could go running through the room, Maria sprayed out the flames with water. The manager slumped to the floor sobbing. Maria tossed the almost empty shampoo bottle at him and turned for the door.

"That," she said. "Is vanity's price."

With a smile, she fished out the second bottle and drove toward Chase's home.

35

# *Diamonds are Forever*

*T*hey're dropping like flies, I tell ya."

"Sure they are, Ma."

I rolled my eyes and glanced out the window. Mom and I were chatting in the family room of the Serene Acres Retirement Community.

"Don't you roll your eyes at me, young lady."

A sigh slipped out before I could catch it. I swallowed a groan. Now I was in for it.

"You listen here…"

A bony finger shook in my face. Blue hair bounced around a perfectly made up face. I slumped lower in the overstuffed chair and spoke before she really got going.

"Look, Ma. Sorry. Go ahead and tell me what's going on."

Her hand dropped to her lap. She paused to rearrange her thoughts before she spoke again. Finally, she looked me dead in the eye and spoke in a breathless whisper.

"People are dying around here."

Laughter bubbled up inside me. I cleared my throat, to cover the giggles.

"Uh…Ma, this is a nursing home."

"This is a retirement community!"

"Connected to a nursing home. I think you gotta expect a certain number of the inmat…uh…residents to expire."

Mom flopped back in her chair disgusted with me. I leaned over and picked up a flyer from the end table. Diamonds are Forever, it said. Before I could open it, Ma dropped her bombshell.

"I just don't think I can stay here any longer."

I shot forward in my chair the flyer forgotten in my hand. If Mom left Serene Acres, she'd move back in with me. Oh, God. I grabbed my tea glass and tried to compose myself. I snuck a look at Ma. She was smirking. I swallowed a sigh.

"What makes you think too many people are dying around here, Ma?"

"They hauled Mattie Jacobs out of here at four-thirty this morning."

"Ma, Mattie Jacobs was ninety-eight years old."

"And healthy as a twenty year old. We played penny a point gin till two o'clock this morning."

"How much she into ya for, Ma?"

"That doesn't have anything to do with it."

I grinned and put down my glass.

"Ma, did it ever occur to you that Mattie might just have died of old age."

She glared. "How long was I on the waiting list before I got in here?"

"I don't know, two, three years."

"You know how long the waiting list is now?"

I shrugged.

"There isn't one."

"I still don't see anything sinister going on, Ma."

She shook her head at me in disgust. I centered my empty glass on the coaster and stood.

"I gotta get out of here, Ma. I'll be back to see you in a couple of days." I hitched my purse over my shoulder and started toward the door with Mom at my heels.

"Call before you come over, you know how I hate people just dropping by."

"I will, Ma."

I pushed open the door and she stopped me with a hand on my elbow. Her fingers trembled.

"I wish you'd check into this for me, Libby. Something's going on around here."

Her voice was so soft we couldn't possibly be overheard, but she looked furtively over her shoulder anyway.

"I'll see what I can find out, Ma."

She smiled, patted my arm and turned away. I wondered if I'd imagined the trembling fingers.

I tossed my purse on the passenger seat of my Honda Civic and noticed I still clutched the diamond flyer. I stuffed it in my oversized bag and headed out of the parking lot. It was unlike Mom to worry. Mostly she complained about the food or the staff. Maybe she was just upset over losing her friend Mattie.

I drove on through town and braked in front of my house. Sparkles, my big fluffy almost white cat met me at the door proudly carrying something in his mouth.

"What ya got there Spark?"

He gently placed his treasure at my feet and looked up at me. It was a big, faceted crystal bead that I'd removed from an old piece of jewelry. I planned to use it in a new piece I was working on. I scooped it off the floor and rubbed Sparkles behind the ears.

"Spark, you've got to quit stealing my beads. I need those."

He burbled and rubbed his head under my hand. I laughed and went into my workroom to replace the bead.

Sparkles has an affinity for anything that glitters. That's how he got his name. I thought I had everything put away where he couldn't get to it. He'd managed to paw open the drawer to get to his glittering toy. Guess I was going to have to install baby locks to keep him out.

Sparkles helped me read the newspaper while I ate lunch. I noticed four local nursing homes advertising openings. That was unusual, but it didn't mean people were being murdered. Probably just a normal cycle.

Sparkles lost interest in the paper and started rooting around in my purse. I shooed him away and turned the page. I heard him get back in my purse. A minute later, he walked across the paper with the diamond flyer in his mouth and sat down on the sports page. Reading the newspaper with a cat is always a challenge.

"Sparks, get off the paper."

He dropped the flyer and flopped down, rolled over to make the newspaper crinkle and stuck all four feet in the air. I laughed and rubbed his tummy. He nipped at my hand and I jerked back.

"Sparks, what's got into you?"

He rolled to his feet and batted the flyer toward me. As soon as I picked it up, he hopped down to look for a snack.

It was an eye-catching pamphlet. The first two pages showed photos of beautiful diamond jewelry. I wondered briefly, why the jewelry store owners were targeting Serene Acres. It wasn't exactly a haven for geriatric millionaires. I flipped the page and found a list of crematorium prices. Confused, I looked at the back page. Printed across the bottom was, Compliments of Pleasant Dreams Mortuary. Now I was really confused. I turned back to the beginning of the flyer and started to read.

Apparently, the crematorium captured the carbon as they cremated your loved one, then pressed the carbon into diamonds. My lip curled at the thought as I read on. Depending on the size of the deceased and the size of your wallet, they could make several small stones or one large one. Eeeuw. Who'd want to wear jewelry made of dead people? I dropped the flyer on the table and shook my head. Yuck.

Since I'd sort of promised Ma I'd look into the dwindling senior population, I figured I should make an effort. She was bound to call me later and ask what I'd found out. I told Sparks goodbye and drove to Washington Manor. My good friend Susan Adams worked in the office there. She grinned up from her desk when I poked my head in.

"What are you doing here?" she asked.

"Just stopped by to chat."

"Well, you picked a good time, I'm getting ready to go home. Want to go get a drink somewhere?"

"Sure."

"Give me just a sec and I'll meet you out front."

I walked outside and sat down on a bench. The sun was warm on my face. I closed my eyes and relaxed.

"Hey there."

I jumped and looked at my bench mate. He was ninety if he was a day and there wasn't a tooth in his head. I smiled and said hello.

"They're killing us off in here," he said.

"What?"

"Yep, two or three a week. I don't care about myself, but some of them young pups better watch out."

"Uh...right."

He scooted closer to me and put his hand on my thigh. I cringed and leaned away.

"Somebody's makin money off this, mark my words."

"Off killing senior citizens?"

He squeezed my leg and gave it a pat.

"That's right honey, it's always about money."

"Of course."

Susan pushed through the door and I jumped to my feet.

"Hey, detective," she said. "It's time for you to go back inside. Dinner's almost ready."

He got up and shuffled toward the door.

"Follow the money," he yelled over his shoulder. "It's always about the money."

He disappeared inside and I looked at Suze.

"Who is that guy?" I asked.

"Just one of our residents. He used to be a police detective. Now he goes around telling everybody how to solve crimes. He's harmless. We took away his gun."

She laughed and headed for her car. I followed her to Boot's Bar and Grill. We slipped into a booth in the rear and ordered beer and nachos.

"So what case is your pet senior detective working on now?" I asked as I took a slug of my draft. I had a sneaking suspicion I already knew.

"Oh, this week he's convinced someone is killing off the residents."

"I was afraid of that."

Susan paused with a nacho halfway to her mouth and asked me what was wrong.

"Mom is convinced of the same thing." I took a gulp of my beer. "Suze, what if they're right."

"You can't take the detective seriously, Lib. Last month he was convinced someone was dealing drugs from the kitchen."

"Didn't they bust one of your aides for dealing pot a few weeks ago?"

Susan went still and stared at me.

"I never really made that connection," she said.

"It was probably just coincidence."

"But what if it wasn't. Libby, we are at 50% capacity right now. That's the lowest in ten years. It's why I went home early today. I'm out of paperwork. Can you believe that?"

I nursed my beer and tried to come up with a reason to knock off old folks while Susie spouted theories. The people in the adjoining booth started looking at us funny. We must have sounded like lunatics. Probably it was time to go home. Before Suze could order another beer, I herded her out the door to my car.

As usual, Sparkles met us at the door. Instead of a new sparkling treasure, he was carrying the diamond flyer. Suze took it from him and dropped into one of my kitchen chairs. I snagged two beers from the fridge and sat down across from her. Susie drank the beer and flipped through the flyer. She finished reading and slapped it on the table.

"That's just morbid," she said.

"What, making jewelry out of deceased family members?"

"It's sick."

"I don't know. The idea is kind of growing on me. Maybe I'll get a pair of earrings made when Mom dies."

"Libby!"

I laughed. "I was joking."

We migrated to the living room and settled in for some girl talk. As we neared the end of my beer supply, the conversation came back to Mom and the Detective.

"Suze, I'd really like to talk to your detective."

"Great, let's go."

Susie hopped off the couch, tripped on the rug and crashed to the floor. Laughing, I stood to help her, stumbled over Sparkles and wound up on top of her. We dissolved into helpless laughter as we untangled ourselves. Sparkles stalked out in a huff. We decided it might be better to visit the detective sober.

Eyes squeezed shut, I pressed one hand against my head and mumbled hello into the telephone. It was six a.m.

"Libby, this is your mother."

I jerked as the voice on the phone pierced my brain.

"Hi, Ma. Can't this wait until later?"

"No, I need you over here right now. I want out of here today."

"Ma, it's six in the morning and I think I'm dying."

"Libby, I want out of this place."

The phone crashed in my ear and I groaned. Susie was sitting up on the couch. Her red hair was flat on one side and sticking straight out on the other. She looked as bad as I felt.

"Who was that," she mumbled.

"Ma."

"What's she want at this hour?"

"She wants me to bring her home. Says she's leaving Serene Acres."

"You'll kill each other before you make it a week."

With that pronouncement, she stumbled off the couch. A minute later, I heard the shower start. I made a pot of turbocharged coffee and swallowed two Tylenol. When Susie came out of the bathroom, I handed her a cup and shuffled to the bathroom. By the end of my shower, I was fairly certain my hangover wasn't terminal. I couldn't tell yet about Suze.

I suggested we go see the detective before we picked up Ma from Serene Acres. Suze just nodded and followed me out to the car.

The detective was sunning himself on the bench out front when we pulled up. I invited him to breakfast and with a big toothless grin, he crawled in the back seat.

At Denny's, I slipped into the booth across from the detective. Suze sat down next to him. The waitress brought coffee and took our order. I waited until she left, then asked my question.

"Detective, what makes you think people are killing off nursing home patients?"

"Money," he said.

"Could you elaborate a little bit?"

"It's always about money."

I sighed. Susie bit back a smile and sipped her coffee. She was starting to feel better. I tried again.

"Okay, if someone were killing off the nursing home patients, how would they profit from it?"

He sat with his eyes closed, not moving. I looked at Suze and she shrugged. When he hadn't moved for several minutes, I poked his arm to make sure he was still alive.

"Detective?"

He snapped his eyes open and glared at me.

"I'm thinking."

"Oh, sorry."

He closed his eyes and thought some more. Suze and I sat just staring at each other. The waitress stepped into the silence and brought our breakfast. The detective opened his eyes, picked up his fork and dug in. I wondered if he'd forgotten the question.

"Do the dead people have families?" He finally asked.

"What?"

He turned and looked at Susan.

"Young lady, can you find out how many of the recent dead folks have families?"

"Uh. Well, sure."

"Then do it."

He finished his last bite of egg, wiped his mouth on a napkin and glanced down at his watch.

"It's time for The Price is Right. I need to get back."

I nodded and we headed to the parking lot. I dropped Susan and the detective off at Boot's so she could pick up her car. She promised to check out the family angle and give me a call. My next stop was Serene Acres. Ma was waiting at the door when I drove up. She trotted across the sidewalk with her overnight bag and got in the passenger side before I could get out.

"What are you doin', Ma?"

"I'm leaving. I told you that this morning."

"You can't just leave, Ma."

"I can and I am and that's that."

I sighed and drove to the house. Sparkles met us at the door with the diamond flyer. Mom took it from him and sat down in the living room. She glared at me when I walked in with a glass of tea.

"You're not thinking about doing this to me, are you?"

"Of course not, Ma. I just picked it up at Serene Acres yesterday."

"Well, I won't have it, you understand. I don't want to be made into a cheap piece of jewelry."

"They're not really that cheap, Ma."

"I won't have it, Libby."

I grinned. "Relax, Ma. I'm not going to kill you off for a new pair of earrings..."

I stood up from the couch and snatched the flyer from her hands. Mom looked at me in surprise as I started flipping through it.

"I gotta go, Ma. I'll be back. Feed Sparkles, would you."

I grabbed my purse and ran out the door. Susan was walking out of the nursing home when I slid to a stop out front.

"Get in."

She slid in next to me and I wheeled away, I didn't say a word until we parked down the block next to the softball field.

"What did you find out, Suze?"

"We've had twenty-two deaths in the last six months. Six of them were expected natural deaths due to illness. Only those six have family in the area."

I raised my eyebrows at that, but she wasn't finished.

"I compared it to the previous six months. We only lost five residents. All of them natural expected deaths. I think someone is killing these people, Libby."

"Can you get the same information from Serene Acres?" I asked.

"I'll get it. We've got to stop these people."

"I'm going to check out something else. I'll drop you off at your car and we can meet back there in an hour or so. We'll talk to the detective again then."

After I dropped Susan at her car, I drove across town to visit the Pleasant Dreams Mortuary. A quiet voiced gentleman in a dark suit met me at the door. I told him I was looking into funeral arrangements for my mother and we spent the next forty minutes discussing arrangements and cost. I asked about the diamonds and his face lit with pleasure as he described the process.

"Due to new developments in the process, the cost is very reasonable. Just six months ago, the cost was prohibitive. The making of the diamond alone was over four thousand dollars. Now we can do it for much less and sell the jewels for less than four hundred."

"Four hundred dollars?"

"Well for a small diamond. Of course the price for a karat or more is still around a thousand, but that's very reasonable."

"Well thank you, I'll let you know what I decide."

"We have a very attractive prepayment plan if you're interested."

"Well, thanks. I'll let you know."

His eyes gleamed as he felt the time to close the sale draw near. I backed out of his office and moved quickly toward the door. Before I stepped outside, I asked one more question.

"Could this be done to someone without their family being made aware of it?"

The sparkle faded from his eyes and his face grew stony.

"Ma'am, that would be unethical."

He pulled the door closed and latched it firmly behind me. Guess I'd touched a nerve. As I pulled out of the drive, I saw him staring out the window at me. He was talking on his cell phone. I shivered.

I joined Susan and the detective in the day room for a cup of coffee.

"Was it the same story at Serene Acres?" I asked.

Her eyes gave me the answer before she nodded.

"What do you think?" I asked the detective.

"Follow the money, without money, you seldom have murder."

"I think I've figured out the money angle." I said, then I filled them in on what I'd learned at the mortuary.

Our toothless detective grinned and patted my knee.

"If they are selling the diamonds for a thousand a karat, then it can't be costing them more than a hundred to make them. The mark up on diamonds is astronomical," he said. "So far they've only murdered people without families. They'll get greedy before long and then none of us will be safe."

"We've got to stop them, Lib," Susan said.

A chair scooted behind me. I jumped and looked over my shoulder. An orderly quickly turned away and started wiping off an already clean table. I was sure he'd been listening to our conversation.

"Detective, maybe you should come home with me until we figure out what's going on."

"Nonsense. I can take care of myself."

He patted my head and headed back to his room. The orderly straightened from the table he was cleaning and watched him walk down the hall. I motioned Susan toward the door and we left in my car.

"What should we do now, I asked as I drove?"

"They have to be selling those diamonds somewhere. Let's go jewelry shopping at that new store, The Diamond Mine."

We turned out of the parking lot and headed downtown. The Diamond Mine building was blinding white with navy trim around the doors and windows. Diamonds glittered against the navy backdrop in the windows.

Inside was a fantasyland of diamonds in every size and shape. Set into jewelry, watches and table decorations. They even had a sweater with a snowflake design highlighted with diamonds. The lighting in the store was perfect and the facets flashed and glowed in turns. The sales clerk met us at the door with a smile of welcome.

I headed straight for the sweater and trailed my fingers over the design. The clerk hovered at my shoulder as I flipped over the price tag.

"Is this price correct?" I asked.

He flashed his bright smile. "Most of our diamonds are manufactured. New developments in the process have made them very reasonable."

His pitch was eerily similar to the mortuary guy's. I hoped he couldn't read anything in my expression.

"I bet DeBeers isn't crazy about that," I said.

He moved away and rearranged some items in one of his display cases without answering. I slipped my checkbook out, checked the balance, and sighed. I would have loved to have that sweater.

Susan browsed and I asked how the diamonds were made. I got a couple of vague friendly answers. When I asked about diamonds made from human cremains, he got decidedly unfriendly. I scooted Suze toward the door, we'd worn out our welcome. Looking back over my shoulder, I saw the sales clerk jabbing buttons on his cell phone as the door closed behind us.

I called my cousin at city hall when we got back to the house. In minutes, I'd found out that Pleasant Dreams Mortuary and the Diamond Mine were owned by the same people. I dropped the phone in the cradle and told Susan and Mom what I'd learned.

"You need to go to the police with this, Libby," Mom said.

"With what, Ma. That the same people own the mortuary and the jewelry store, or that people are starting to die off at nursing homes. The cops would laugh me out of their office. We don't have any proof that anyone's committing a crime."

"I still think you should call, Lib."

"They'd laugh me out of town. I think I will go hang out with the detective, though. Did you see that orderly hovering around us this afternoon, Suze?"

Her eyes widened.

"Do you think the detective might be in danger?" asked Suze.

"I think we shouldn't take any chances."

I patted Sparkles on the head and headed back to the nursing home. I located the detective in the TV room and he agreed to hide me. His eyes glittered as I wedged myself into his closet. He was enjoying this.

After what seemed like hours, I heard his going to bed sounds, then the lights went out. My legs were starting to cramp and I was beginning to think my whole idea was nuts when I heard someone shuffle into the room. I peeked through the louvers in the door. The orderly from the dayroom lifted the detective's arm and tried to shove in a needle. Before I could move, the old guy exploded off the bed in a flurry of skinny arms and legs. The orderly smacked him on the head as I burst out of the closet. The detective went limp and the orderly turned toward me. I was unarmed and untrained in fighting of any kind, so I took a deep breath and prepared to scream. Before the noise got past my throat, the orderly clapped his hand over my mouth and twisted my arm up behind me. The strangled noise I managed didn't make it past his hand.

"Don't make any noise, doll."

He gave my arm a vicious twist.

"I'm going to let you go and you are not going to move, right?"

I nodded.

He let go and I sprang for the door. Pain exploded in my head and everything went black.

I woke tied to a gurney in a clean, brightly lit room. A small door was set into the wall near my feet. On a high shelf around the room were cremation urns. I swallowed once, took a deep breath and turned my head. The detective was lying limp next to me. I hoped he wasn't dead.

"Detective," I whispered.

His eyes opened and he grinned. My breath whooshed out in relief.

"I think we got 'em worried now, kid," he said.

"Yeah, we really got 'em on the run, detective."

He snickered.

I rolled my eyes and frantically tried to work my wrists free of the ties. To my surprise, my right hand slipped loose. I looked at it in disbelief. "Don't just sit there, untie me," the detective snapped

I unhooked my left arm, scrambled to the detective and did the same for him. When he was free, he laid the ties back over his arms so he still looked secure.

"What are you doing?" I whispered. "Let's get out of here."

"We got to stop 'em."

"No one knows where we are. We've gotta get out of this place."

He stubbornly shook his head. I wanted to run out the door, but if the old guy was staying, I couldn't just leave. I lay back down and arranged the ties over my arms. Just as I finished, the door opened and the mortuary attendant walked in.

I turned my head toward him.

"You should have kept your nose out of things," he said to me.

I couldn't have agreed more.

"I'm going to give you a close personal lesson on the first stage of diamond making."

He jerked open a door in the wall by my feet and rolled the gurney with the detective toward it. My stomach contracted. He was going to cremate the detective and then me. Yikes.

"The first step is the cremation," he continued. "Unfortunately you won't be around for step two."

He turned toward me and grinned.

While his back was turned, my toothless friend leaped from his gurney and slammed it into the guy's legs. I leapt from my perch and looked frantically around for a weapon. A brass cremation urn was on a table. I swung it at the head of our captor as he struggled to his feet. It hit with a solid thunk and he slithered to the floor.

Grinning, the detective grabbed my hand and we raced toward the door. We slid to a stop, as it swung open. In walked the orderly and the jewelry store attendant. The orderly had a gun. He waved it in our direction and we stepped back. He moved toward us and raised the barrel as the door crashed open again. He swung around at the noise and found a police officer standing in the doorway. I sagged with relief.

The officer stepped in as the orderly dropped his gun to the floor. Two detectives followed him into the room and Mom and Suze ducked in behind them.

I dropped into the nearest chair as the detectives started snapping on handcuffs. My toothless buddy slipped his arm across my shoulders and planted a kiss on my cheek.

"You done good, girly."

"How'd they know we were here?" I asked.

"You don't think I'd set up a sting operation without backup, do you?"

"I never gave it a thought. How'd Mom and Suze get involved?"

One of the detectives looked up and grinned.

"They came down to the station and we couldn't get rid of them," he said.

"Ma grinned and nodded her head toward the nicest looking detective and raised her eyebrows at me."

I shook my head and laughed.

"So, you're moving back to Serene Acres. Right, Ma?"

"I don't know. I kind of enjoyed being home today."

I groaned and rubbed the aching knot on the back of my head. Susan had the nerve to laugh.

# Socks

He walked out of Gleason's Department Store clutching a plastic carrier bag filled with socks. Not special socks, just ordinary white crew socks with cushion soles. 'The finest work socks made,' he'd been assured by the sales clerk. He was quite pleased with his purchase. It was the first time he'd ever bought socks.

He pondered how a forty-two year old man got to be that age without ever purchasing a pair of socks. First his mom bought his socks. Then, Uncle Sam bought socks, after that his wife bought socks. Now, Gordon Lewis, ex marine, ex cop, and ex husband, was buying his own socks. And doing a damn fine job of it if he did say so himself. He smiled as he walked down the street.

His sock reverie was broken by the familiar report of a high powered rifle. He heard the zing of the bullet, saw concrete fragments explode off the sidewalk and observed a pedestrian gasp in pain and surprise, grasp his arm and stumble to his knees. He glanced in the direction of the shot and zeroed in on the upper floor of the old Roxiam building. Sunlight refracted off something in the far left window, then disappeared. A rifle scope. Gordon glanced at the injured pedestrian; assured himself he wasn't badly hurt, and raced toward the shooter, his plastic bag of socks forgotten on the sidewalk.

Car horns blared as he dodged across the street. He burst through the door scattering a clutch of office workers staring out the window, raced to the stairs and took them two at a time. He arrived at the fourth floor barely breathing hard and reached instinctively for the service revolver at his side only belatedly realizing it wasn't there. He wasn't a cop anymore.

Glancing left and right, he slipped out of the stairwell, looked toward the elevator, and swore quietly under his breath when he saw it was on the ground floor. He'd gotten there too late. Moving quickly down the hall, he paused outside the door where he was sure the shooter had been. The knob turned easily in his hand. He pressed his back against the wall and pushed the door open with his foot. No shots greeted him from inside. He hadn't really expected any.

Stepping through the doorway, he took two steps inside and stopped. The room was empty. The floor was covered with a coating of dust and foot prints were clear leading to the window and back. The lower right pane was missing from the window. Broken shards of glass glittered in the sunlight coming from the window and a shell casing from a 30-30 lay in shadow against the wall. A piece of paper skittered across the floor in the breeze from the broken window. He slipped the cell phone from his pocket and called Detective Arden.

"This is Gordon, you've got a shooter downtown," he said.

"Tell me somethin' I don't know, Gord."

"I found his perch."

"Where are you, I'm on my way."

Gordon told him and waited for Len Arden to show up. Len used to be his partner and was still trying to get him back on the force. A siren whined down the street and stopped close by. A few minutes later, a portly detective in an ill fitting sport coat wheezed up the stairs.

"Why don't the elevators ever work in these old buildings?" he gasped.

"You ought to lay off the donuts, Lenny."

Ignoring the jibe, he hitched his pants over his oversized hips as he walked over to join Gordy.

"Show me what ya got, Gord."

Gordon stepped to the open door, pointed to the broken window and the shell casing on the floor.

"Looks like we might have a note or it could just be some trash." He added.

Noises came from the stairwell and two uniforms joined them outside the shooters perch. The detective called in a crime scene team, told the uniforms to keep everyone else off the top floor and leaned back against the wall to wait. Gordon squatted on his heels beside him.

"Get me photos and a size on the shoe prints," Len said when the crime scene team arrived. "Bag the shell casing and that piece of paper then I'll get out of your hair and let you work."

They did as he asked and handed him the bagged piece of paper. He read it and handed it to Gordon. The note was pieced together out of cut out letters, Gordon thought, then looked closer. They weren't cut out letters. They were made on a computer to look like cut out letters. A sniper with an artistic bent. He read the note, 'Gordon, it could have been you'. He paused in thought, read it through again and handed it back to the detective.

"Who'd you piss off, Gord?" Lenny asked.

"Nobody wants to shoot me, Len," he said.

"Somebody does."

Gordon shook his head and turned to go downstairs. Lenny spoke with the crime scene techs and followed Gordon out of the building.

"Let me buy you a cup of coffee, Gord."

"I don't know anything about this, Lenny."

"Then I'll buy you a cup of coffee for old time sake."

Gordon shrugged and followed Lenny down the street to Lucy's Java Palace. The sidewalk and pavement were littered with dirty socks. The wind tumbled the plastic carrier bag across his path. Gordon snagged it and found inside, one perfect pair of socks. He sighed with frustration over his ruined purchase as he ducked through Lucy's doorway. She waved from the counter as he slid into a booth. Lenny slid in across from him. They ordered coffee. Gordon snorted when the detective ordered a donut.

"Shut up, Gordon."

Gordon hid a smile behind his coffee cup.

They discussed possible motives for a shooter but after an hour and another donut they didn't have any ideas. Lenny picked up the check and they walked back outside. As they made their way down the sidewalk the sharp rifle report sounded again. Detective Arden grunted and stumbled to the ground. Blood blossomed at the shoulder of the ill fitting sport coat as he groaned.

Gordon keyed Lenny's radio, called in an officer down and their location. He dropped his plastic bag for the second time and raced for the alley between the styling salon and the bar down the street. A shadow disappeared around the corner as he skidded into the alley. He raced to the end and looked both ways. There was no one in sight, just a piece of paper being tossed about by the breeze. He picked it up by the corner. The style was the same as the first, only the message was different. 'I'm getting closer, Gordon.'

Footsteps pounded up behind him. He turned to the two uniforms and shook his head.

"Too late."

They holstered their weapons. He handed them the note and told them about the first one. They walked a grid in the alley and finally found a shell casing lying underneath a tired looking rose bush. One of the uniforms dropped the casing into an evidence bag. Gordon walked back up the street as they were loading Lenny into an ambulance.

"Did you get him?" Lenny asked.

Gordon shook his head.

"You gonna be okay?" he asked.

Lenny nodded and hissed through his teeth as the stretcher jolted into the back of the ambulance. After the ambulance pulled away, Gordon looked around for his last pair of socks but his shopping bag was nowhere to be found. He shrugged and started back up the street to Gleason's for another round of socks.

His mind was on those notes. Who was behind this? It didn't make any sense. He'd made some collars but they were mostly small time crooks with small jail time to go with it. Nothing anybody'd carry a grudge about. He walked past Gleason's without noticing it, still wondering why someone would try to shoot him.

A thought niggled at the back of his mind. Something his ex wife had said a couple of weeks back. What was it? Something she was worried about. Money? No that wasn't it. Something she was afraid of? Maybe.

He shook his head in frustration. He couldn't remember. He hadn't been paying much attention. Mary was so beautiful. How'd he ever manage to screw things up so bad that she'd left? "I'll bet she never lost the socks before she got home with them," he muttered. Mary only lost socks in the washing machine. At the thought of socks he looked up, realized he'd missed Gleason's and turned to walk back down the street. He was going batty.

At Gleason's he headed back to the sock department and took a quick look around to see if the same sales clerk was working. He hoped not. It'd be hard to explain what he'd done with a dozen pairs of socks in a couple of hours. He made it to the sock department and was sorting out a few pair when the clerk popped up beside him.

"Back for more?" he asked. "Boy, you must really like socks."

Gordon stifled a groan. This just wasn't his day. He picked out six pair and the clerk walked through the store with them to the register. Gordon followed slowly behind, still working away at what he'd forgotten about his conversation with Mary. Nothing was coming, he was losing his memory. He sighed in frustration, leaned against the check out counter and stared out the window.

Police cars cruised up and down the street. Officers on foot stopped pedestrians, and questioned shop keepers. He itched to be out there with them trying to run down the shooter. Not for the first time he questioned his reasons for leaving the force. He reached back unconsciously to rest his hand on the butt of his revolver and rolled his eyes when it wasn't there. He still felt naked without it.

As he pulled out his wallet to pay for the socks, the front window of Gleason's exploded in a shower of glass. The clerk shrieked and dove under the counter. Gordon covered his face against the glass, then glanced at the rooftops across the street. A fleeing figure disappeared from sight. He shouted to the nearest officer as he ran out the door and they dodged through traffic together. They split up around the building but no one was moving between the buildings or in the alley behind.

Gordon stood in the alley waiting for the officers to come back down from the roof. Knowing beforehand what they would find, another shell casing, another note. What the hell was going on?

Money. Mary. The two words shifted back and forth in his mind. Why was he stuck on that theme? He crouched next to the wall, pulled a cigarette from the pack in his pocket and cupped his hands around the match to get it lit. He shoved the matches back in his shirt pocket and saw the check peeking out. Alimony.

Money. Mary.

"That's it," he shouted.

The cop sharing his space in the alley turned to look at him in surprise.

"I know who the shooter is," he said.

The cop called Arden's replacement and they met again at Lucy's, Gordon looking carefully around trying to spot the shooter. He didn't show himself.

They sat at a back booth and the detective pulled the newest note out of an inside pocket. This one said, 'I could have had you that time, Gordon'.

"It's my ex wife's new boyfriend." Gordon told the detective. "She told me a couple of weeks ago he was really starting to scare her. I didn't pay much attention but one thing she said stuck in my mind. She told me that just the sight of the alimony check with my name on it sent him into a rage." Gordon smiled. "I offered to stop sending them if she thought that would help."

The detective laughed then asked Gordon for his ex wife's name, address and work number. He gave them out, shrugged off the detective's offer of protection and told him goodbye.

In Lucy's after the detective left, he sat. Away from the windows, shielded from gunfire by the high back of the booth he finished his coffee and pondered the best way to get home without getting shot. Nothing came immediately to mind so he had another cup of coffee. When he reached for his wallet to leave a tip, he realized it was still at Gleason's with his second failed attempt to acquire socks. He dug in his pockets, came up with enough to cover the coffee and headed back to Gleason's.

Workmen were boarding up the front window with a piece of plywood when he got there. The lights inside were off and the front door was locked. This wasn't his day for socks. He gazed down at the bare ankle showing beneath the hem of his jeans and shook his head.

The shots were getting closer he thought. The guy doesn't want to take me out long distance. He's just playing. When it gets serious it's gonna be one on one. He looked around and scanned the faces of the people walking down the street. He didn't know what Mary's boyfriend looked like, didn't even know his name. Mostly he liked to pretend he didn't exist. Guess that wasn't going to work anymore.

He walked slowly down the street to his apartment. A police cruiser stopped beside him and offered a ride. He climbed in on the passenger side and asked about Lenny. Lenny was going to be fine, the officer told him. He got out in front of his building and checked the hallway. It was clear. He slipped his key in the lock and closed the door behind him with a click. Before he could lock it something moved in his peripheral vision. He dove at the shadow and they hit the ground with a thud.

"Ow, you big oaf. You trying to kill me, or what?"

Gordon stopped and looked into Mary's face. She was on the floor under him and she was smiling. He leaned down and kissed her. He'd have kept the kiss going but she squirmed and pushed him away. He raised his head and smiled down at her.

"God you're beautiful, Mary."

She smiled, then the look in her eyes changed. "Gordon, he's going to kill you."

"You're boyfriend?"

She nodded.

"Would that bother you?" he asked.

Tears filler her eyes and trickled into her hair.

"Of course it would."

Gordon smiled.

"Then I guess we'd better not let that happen, huh."

He leaned down and kissed her again, then got to his feet and pulled her up with him. She leaned against him and his arms automatically went around her. They were a perfect fit. He looked down into eyes that were still bright with tears and wondered if he had any chance at all at winning her back.

"I've missed you, Gordy," she said.

"Oh, baby. I have missed you too."

He pulled her close and they kissed again, long and deep. He could feel his body responding to her just like always.

"That a gun in your pocket, Gordo, or are you just happy to see me?"

"Come into the bedroom and we'll find out," he said.

"You are a smooth talker."

Gordon scooped her into his arms and took her to the bedroom. Mary slipped into the bathroom to get undressed and Gordon shucked his clothes into a pile on the floor. He was standing in the bedroom sans clothing when Mary stumbled back out into the room followed by a man in dirty Levi's and a black tee shirt. His chin was covered in stubble and his eyes were wild. Gordon's desire wilted in an instant.

"Well," the stranger said. "Isn't this just sweet. You were supposed to pick up the alimony check not jump in the sack."

He twisted Mary's arm up behind her and she moaned in pain and fear. Gordon clamped down on his fury and looked around the room for a weapon. The police academy didn't cover naked combat, neither did the Marines. Mary struggled and her soon to be ex boyfriend chopped the side of her neck with his free hand. She crumpled to the floor and Gordon leaped forward.

The shooter grabbed his rifle where it leaned inside the bathroom door and swung it butt first at Gordon's head. Gordon twisted and took the blow on the shoulder. He tried to grab the rifle but his attacker was too quick.

"Why are you doing this?" Gordon asked.

"She still loves you."

Gordon smiled.

His attacker bent down and lunged forward. Gordon slipped to the side, grabbed the neck of his tee shirt and swung him away. The dark headed man slammed against the dresser but didn't lose the rifle. Gordon started forward and the rifle swung up to point at his chest.

Mary moved on the floor behind their attacker. Gordon carefully kept his gaze on the gunman's face and wished he at least had on his boxers.

Mary reached into the pile of clothes and slowly pulled out his cell phone. He watched without taking his eyes off the gunman's face as she dialed 911 and slid the phone back into the clothing pile.

"Oh, Gordon," she moaned.

"Shut up," shouted the gunman.

"Gordon Lewis," she said very clearly. "Why is he trying to kill you?"

"I said shut up."

He swung the rifle toward her head. She ducked and it hit her on the shoulder. Mary groaned in pain and scooted toward the clothing pile.

"Why would someone try to kill you in your own home," she said.

Gordon hoped the 911 dispatcher was catching on, then he thought of the cops busting through his door and finding him standing naked in his bedroom with his ex wife and her current boyfriend. That wasn't an acceptable resolution to this problem.

The gunman swung the rifle toward Mary.

"If you say one more word I'm going to kill you," he snapped.

Mary started to speak. Gordon shook his head and leapt at the gunman before the rifle swung back his way. He hit him kidney high. The rifle flew out of his grasp and glass tinkled to the pavement below as the gun fell through the window and clattered to the ground. The two men grappled on the floor, both trying to inflict damage. This time, Gordon had the upper hand. It's surprisingly difficult to grab hold of a naked man.

Gordon got one hand behind the gunman's back, slammed him face first to the floor, pulled his arms up behind him and sat down. He was straddling him in that manner when the cops burst into the bedroom.

They came in with guns drawn and stopped, mouths dropping open in surprise. Surprise turned to laughter and Gordon blushed from head to toe. All the cops in the room that day will vouch for it. When their laughter was under control one of them finally relived Gordon of his position atop the gunman. Gordon made a hasty exit to the bathroom. He found a pair of jeans in the dirty laundry, slipped them on and walked back into the bedroom. The cops still in the room greeted him with grins and winks and Gordon groaned in embarrassment. Mary shooed them out of the room then slipped into his arms.

"You're my hero."

"I looked like a pervert."

Mary laughed.

"You're laughing at me."

She laughed harder. Gordon grinned and pulled her close.

"You owe me big time, sweetheart."

She wriggled in his arms.

"I can think of a couple of ways to pay off my debt."

Gordon, embarrassment forgotten, felt his desire returning as Mary turned her face up to be kissed. He was definitely going to get her back, he could just feel it. He kissed her then whispered in her ear.

"You know what I want more than anything?"

"You name it cowboy."

"Could you buy me some socks?"

# Small Town Gossip

**W**hat the hell am I supposed to do with her?"

The her he was speaking of, was me, Robin Walker. The speaker was my new boss, Chief of Police Byron Neuss. I was standing in the corner of the office admiring a framed diploma on the wall. He was whispering to his assistant chief and number one patrol officer, Danny Morton. I glanced over as the chief bellowed again.

"Dammit, Dan.   While I was off recovering from surgery, you was supposed to hire us a qualified police officer. You got us a meter maid. This town don't even have parking meters."

I glanced up at this and rolled my eyes. Danny caught my look and coughed to cover a laugh.

"Chief, she was an Army MP. I don't think she'll have any problems."

The chief went on as if he didn't hear.

"This department is going to hell in a hand basket. I guess she'll be taking off sick when it's that time of the month and just about when we get her trained she'll get hitched and start havin' babies and quit."

I couldn't stifle a laugh. Danny ran his hands over his face and looked an apology my way as he motioned me forward.

"Chief, let me introduce you. Robin, this is Chief Neuss. Chief, Robin Walker, our newest patrol officer."

The Chief stood as I approached and automatically reached to doff the Stetson he usually wore. It was on the hat rack next to the door, so he ran his hand over his thinning silver hair instead. He was maybe five-nine in his high-heeled Tony Lamas. His belly hung over a worn silver rodeo buckle that failed to keep his pants from drooping over his non-existent behind. A fresh surgical scar peaked out above the snaps on his crisp western shirt. He looked unwell, pale and thin except for the paunch.

"Please to meet you, ma'am."

"Nice to meet you, too, sir."

My right arm twitched as I stifled the instinct to salute. Danny noticed and smirked. I wondered how long before I broke that habit.

"I'm right pleased to have you on the force, young lady. Sander's Creek doesn't have much crime, so you rest easy, I'm sure you'll be plenty safe, but just to make sure, I'm gonna put you on patrol with Officer Morton, here."

I raised an eyebrow at Danny.

"Uh, chief, if we ride together, that kinda eliminates the benefit of having another officer on the street."

The chief's face got red and a flush stained his cheeks, making him look more unwell than ever.

"You countermanding my order, son?"

Danny snapped to attention.

"No, sir. Officer Walker rides with me, sir."

I saw his right arm twitch. Danny'd been a civilian for almost ten years. Apparently, saluting's a habit you never break. I knelt down to pick up an ink pen from the floor so the chief wouldn't catch my smile. I stood and handed him the pen. He broke his glare from Danny and smiled.

"Why thank you, young lady." Then he turned to Danny.

"You get out there and get to work. Show this young lady the ropes and make sure she...uh, you all don't get in any trouble."

"Yes, sir."

Danny lost his fight against instinct and snapped off a salute. It was all I could do not to follow suit. We spun on our heels and marched out of the office with military precision. As the door closed behind us, Danny started to apologize.

I waved it away. "Danny, if I took offense at stuff like that, I wouldn't have applied for this job."

"I'm still sorry. The chief's a little old fashioned, I guess. Come on, we'll get the car and I'll give you the grand tour of Sander's Creek."

We drove around town, Danny pointing out places of interest along the way, the Dairy Bell, the high school, Big Jim's bar and grill, the welding school and the Dreamer's Motel. Sander's Creek was slightly bigger than Mayberry. It had six cops not counting the chief. Three on each shift, two on patrol, and one at the station. One of their officers had just left to join the highway patrol, that's why there was an opening for me. I looked around at the tiny burg as we drove and wondered why they needed six cops.

Danny broke the silence as he turned around in the motel parking lot and started back through town.

"How'd you end up coming to Sander's Creek?"

"My grandmother, Betty Stillwell, died a few months back and left me her house. I was getting ready to get out of the service and figured this was as good a place as any to park for a while."

Some unseen barrier released when he found out I had a connection to a local resident.

"Is that right? I didn't realize Miz Betty was your grandma. We'll have to make sure people in town know that you're Miz Betty's granddaughter. They're a little slow to take to strangers around here, but you, well, you're practically a local."

I'd never been to Sander's Creek in my life. Mama hadn't spoken to her mother since before I was born. I'd never even met the woman. But if Danny wanted everyone in town to know that Miz Betty was my grandma, I couldn't see the harm in it.

Now as we drove, Danny related tidbits about the people we passed. Apparently being almost a local entitled me to all the gossip. A little before noon, we nosed into a parking lot filled with cars. There was no sign on the outside of the building, but I could see tables scattered across the inside as we made our way to the front door.

"This is Glen's." Danny said.

He pushed through the door and was hailed with greetings from all sides. Chatter and the sound of cutlery on crockery bounced off the hard floor and walls until I stepped through the door. Then, total silence blanketed the room. I glanced around to find every eye in the place pinned on me.

"Hey everybody," Danny said. "I'd like you to meet our new patrol officer, Robin Walker."

No one moved. I glanced around the room and fought the urge to run out the door. I'd faced men with guns that didn't unnerve me as much. When a plate crashed to the floor in the kitchen, I jumped. Danny pulled me forward and spoke again.

"Robin is Miz Betty's granddaughter."

The silence broke with a roar. People stopped staring. The sound of forks against plates filled the air. Several people got up, introduced themselves and shook my hand. A gentleman Danny introduced as the mayor patted my back and told me how sorry he was about Miz Betty and how glad they were to have me in Sander's Creek. I was overwhelmed.

Danny guided me toward a booth. A waitress brought him an iced tea and asked what I'd like to drink. I told her tea would be fine. She scooted off to get my glass. I glanced around the room and looked back at Danny.

"What the hell was that all about?"

Danny grinned. "I told you they don't really take to strangers around here. I been worrying about how to get you accepted since I hired you. That's the only reason you almost didn't get the job. Would have been nice to know about Miz Betty earlier, it would have been easier on the chief."

I just shook my head. My tea arrived and I took a big gulp.

"The special today is chicken fried steak," the waitress said, looking at Danny.

"That sounds fine, Wynona."

She looked at me and I nodded my agreement. She headed back to the kitchen with our order.

I tapped a fingernail idly against my tea glass and wondered if Sander's Creek had been a big mistake.

We were almost finished eating when Danny's radio burped. He wiped his hands on a napkin and pulled it from his belt.

"Say again, Lou."

"You and the new girl need to get out to the motel and see Miz Marcia. She needs to talk to ya about something."

"Ten-four."

I started to stand. Danny waved me to my seat and finished eating.

"We don't need to get in any hurry. Miz Marcia calls in once a week or so with some complaint or other. Most of the welding school students live out there, so usually she's complaining about loud parties or somebody peeling out of the parking lot. We don't need to get in any hurry."

I shrugged and finished my lunch. Eventually we made our way to the Dreamer's Motel. When we pulled in, an older lady in a worn flowered housedress was pacing around the gravel lot wringing her hands. We got out of the car and I could see tears streaked through her powdered makeup and curls of thin grey hair that had escaped from the bun at her neck.

"Miz Marcia, what's wrong, darlin'?" Danny asked.

She grabbed his arm and started pulling him toward one of the rooms. She was talking so fast I couldn't understand a word.

Danny stopped and put his hand on her shoulder.

"Hon, you need to relax. Take a deep breath and tell me again what happened."

She took a second to compose herself and started over.

"It's one of them boys from the welding school. He's dead."

Danny patted her shoulder and asked which room. She pointed to number eight.

"You stay right here and we'll check it out."

She nodded and stood on the walk beside the building wringing her hands. I followed Danny toward room number eight. The door was slightly ajar.

"Did she say a young man was dead?" I asked.

"Dead drunk more than likely," Danny answered.

He nudged the door open with his foot and looked into the room. I peered over his shoulder and gasped.

"Shit," Danny said.

"I don't think he's drunk," I whispered.

"Welcome to Sander's Creek, Robin."

Danny stepped away from the door and walked toward the owner.

Within twenty minutes, the parking lot of the Dreamer's Motel was full. Besides the cruiser Danny and I had arrived in, there was the chief's suburban, the other cruiser and a couple of pickup trucks. I looked around at the people gathered outside room eight. The Chief, Danny, the dispatcher, the jailer, and all four of the remaining Sander's Creek police officers were in a huddle. This was the biggest crime in Sander's Creek in a hundred years and everyone wanted to get in on the action. I don't know who was minding the cop shop. Guess it didn't really matter. Most of the local residents were lined up on the sidewalk around the parking lot of the motel. If someone needed a cop, they'd know where to find one.

Danny motioned me over.

"Hey, Robin. Take the car and go out to the welding school. Try to find out who this kid's friends were and get statements from the students and faculty. You shouldn't have any trouble getting them to talk to you out there. Most of them are out of towners."

He handed me the keys to the car and a slip of paper with the young man's name written on it, Mark Addison. I tucked the paper in my pocket and angled into the cruiser to drive out to the school. As I pulled out of the lot, the coroners van and the state CSI unit were just turning into the motel.

At the school, I introduced myself to Vickie at the front desk and told her what I needed. She called the instructors to the front and we took over an office while I explained what had happened and what I needed. They told me that Mark was a good student, always showed up on time, worked hard for the most part. When I asked about enemies, they couldn't think of anyone he'd had any kind of disagreement with. They gave me the names of the two students he hung around with the most and I asked if they would send them up to see me first.

While I waited for the two young men to show up, I asked Vickie for copies of attendance records and anything else they had on Mark that might help me learn something about him. She handed me the copies just as the first young man came through the office door.

"Officer, this is Andy Lawton," Vickie said. "Andy, this is Officer Walker. She needs to ask you some questions."

Andy tried to look tough, but beneath his tan, his face had gone pale. He stuffed his hands into his pockets and followed me into the office.

"What's this all about?" he asked.

"Do you know someone named Mark Addison?" I asked.

"Sure. He goes to school here. He's not here today, though. Guess he's sick or hung over or something." He laughed nervously and took a deep breath. "Why you askin' questions about Mark?"

I ignored his question and asked one of my own. "Has Mark got a girlfriend here in town, Andy?"

A smile snuck across his face before he could catch it. He put his serious look on and glanced up at me to see if I'd noticed the smile.

"Yeah, he's dating a local girl. I don't know her name, though."

His eyes slid away from mine as he answered. He shuffled his feet and jammed his hands deeper into his pockets. I wondered why he was lying.

I asked a few more questions, who did Mark hang out with, what was he like, did he do drugs? What was the name of his girlfriend, I asked again, after he'd relaxed a bit.

"Le...uh, like I said. I don't know her name."

I told him that was all I needed for now and asked him to tell Wade Brewer to come in as he left.

He started out the door and turned back. "Ma'am, what's this all about?"

"Mark Addison is dead."

He started to stutter out a question.

"Send Wade in please," I said, ignoring him.

Wade Brewer was young, arrogant and unbelievably good looking for an eighteen-year-old kid. He slouched against the wall in a James Dean pose and gave me a once over. I hid my smile and glanced down at my notebook.

I asked him the same questions I'd posed to Andy and got the same or similar answers. Mark, it appeared, was a good kid. Didn't drink too much, took school pretty seriously, and didn't do drugs. I asked if he had a girlfriend and got the same brief smirk that I'd seen on Andy's face.

"Yeah, he's got a girlfriend."

"Do you know her name?"

Wade shook his head, but the smirk never left his face. I tried to get the information several different ways, but Wade wasn't going to cough up the name, so I let him go and spent the rest of the afternoon talking to the other thirty-five students at the school. After I finished with the last one, I came out of the office and sat down in front of Vickie's desk with a sigh. Four hours of questions and I'd learned nothing.

My radio squawked and I keyed the mic. "This is Walker, go ahead."

"You still at the school?" It was Danny.

"Affirmative."

"Meet me at Glen's as soon as you finish."

"Ten-four."

I snapped the radio back on my belt and rubbed my hands over my face.

"Did you find out anything that will help?" Vickie asked.

"Not yet, but I found out there's something that the boys don't want me to know. I'm hoping that will eventually point me in the right direction. You don't happen to know if Mark had a girlfriend, do you."

"I've heard the guys teasing him about a girl, but you know how boys are, it might have been nothing."

"Where do guys go around here to meet girls? The one's that aren't old enough for the bars."

Vickie laughed. "Would you believe Wal-Mart?"

"Wal-Mart?"

"It's the closest thing to a mall for a hundred miles."

I shook my head as I stood. "Looks like I'm on my way to Wal-Mart. You wouldn't happen to have a photo of Mark, would you?"

Vickie nodded that she did and made me a copy of the photo in his file. I added it to the papers she'd given me earlier and went out to the car. A figure was slouched against the rear fender of my cruiser. He straightened as I approached. It was Andy.

"Ma'am."

"Andy."

"I, uh...wasn't completely truthful with you earlier. I do know the name of Mark's girlfriend. Her first name anyway. It's LeAnn."

I pulled my notebook out and wrote down the name.

"Why the big secret?"

"I, um...I really can't tell you that."

"Andy, I understand you want to keep secrets for a friend. That's admirable, but Mark's dead. He doesn't have any secrets anymore."

"Yes, ma'am. I know, but...I can't say. I really can't. Mark's not the only one that could get in trouble."

"You don't know her last name?" I asked.

"No, ma'am. I'm sorry."

"Can you tell me anything else that might help me find this young lady?"

"She works at Wal-Mart."

I smiled. "Is that were they met?"

Andy nodded. I made another note in my book and thanked Andy for his help. He trotted across the parking lot to an ancient pickup truck and pulled out of the lot before I got my door unlocked.

I drove to Glen's. When I walked in the door, several people nodded and said hello. Danny motioned from a booth in the back and I slid in across from him. I slumped in the booth and rubbed my temples. The waitress, a clone of Wynona named May set a glass of tea on the table in front of me and asked if I was hungry. I ordered a salad and squeezed the lemon into my glass as she went back to fix my order.

"Rough first day," Danny said.

I nodded and took a long pull from my glass. I wished it was a cold beer and said as much to Danny.

"I'll join you in a six-pack after we figure out who shot that kid. You find out anything?"

"I've got something that makes me twitch, but nothing we can really go on, yet."

"Tell me."

"Mark was dating a local girl, LeAnn something. For some reason, the guys he was closest to were really hesitant to tell me her name. Something else is going on with this girl, but I couldn't get anything out of his friends. They weren't talking."

"You think I'd have any luck getting it out of them?" Danny asked.

"You're welcome to try, but I really don't think you're gonna get them to talk."

May showed up with my salad and a cheeseburger and fries for Danny. He started to eat. I pushed the lettuce around in my bowl. He watched me for a while and put down the burger.

"Okay, Walker. Out with it. What's bugging you about this mystery girl?"

"From what I can find out, this kid was a straight arrow. I'm just trying to figure out what kind of trouble a good kid like that can end up in that could get him killed."

"What'd you find out about the girl?"

"Other than her name, just that she works at Wal-Mart."

"Well, if she's about the same age as Mark, her last name is Sinclair. There's another LeAnn out at Wal-Mart, but she's about forty so I think we can rule her out."

"Whatever's going on has something to do with the girl. I tried to get Mark's friend Andy to tell me what it was, but all he said was Mark wasn't the only one that could get hurt if he talked."

Danny dunked a french-fry in his ketchup and pointed it at me as he spoke. "What kind of girl trouble can an eighteen year old kid have that would get him killed?"

"You're a guy, you tell me."

Danny smiled. "I haven't been eighteen in a long time, and I haven't had any girl trouble since my divorce ten years ago."

His eyes crinkled when he smiled, and I noticed they were a blue so dark they were almost black. I bet he had plenty of girl trouble when he was a kid, I thought. He caught me staring and winked. I suddenly found an interest in my salad.

"You get any prints in the kid's room?" I asked to divert his attention.

"Yeah, the state guys are running them through AFIS for us. I'll know if we got any hits later this evening."

"If they don't, we'll have to print all those kids at the school."

"You thinking another student shot this kid?" Danny asked.

"Not really, that's pretty uncharacteristic of a teenager. A kid would be more likely to beat the crap out of him if they thought he was trespassing with their girl."

"We're not making much progress here, Walker. Don't you have any feminine insights?"

70

I laughed. "By the time I was these kids age, I was doing a tour in Korea. I wasn't spending a lot of time dating."

"Hell, I might as well have hired a guy for all the help you are," Danny said.

I laughed. "You know how it is. Everything's a crisis when you're eighteen. Every molehill is a mountain. But maybe we're not giving these kids enough credit. Maybe they really did have a problem they didn't know how to deal with."

"Give me a for instance."

"I don't know, maybe she was pregnant. It's a pretty life changing event under any circumstances, but in a town like this, with all the gossip, it would be awful. No, scratch that, even in Sander's Creek an unwed mother couldn't be that big a deal."

Danny went still as I spoke, his food forgotten on the table in front of him.

"What are you thinking? Danny? You don't think it was someone in her family, do you?"

He closed his eyes and rubbed his temples. "Shit."

"Danny, for God's sake talk to me. You don't think her dad could have done it."

Danny looked up at me and I could read the answer in his eyes before he spoke.

"I'm afraid you might have hit the nail on the head, partner. I guess we'd better go to Wal-Mart. Find out if you're right. I hope to God you're not."

I didn't want to go to Wal-Mart. I didn't want to find out I was right about the killer. I wanted those two kids to go back a couple of days before life got complicated.

With a sigh, I stood and headed toward the parking lot in front of Glen's. Danny followed me out. He slid into the passenger seat, so I tucked in behind the wheel and drove across town to the tiny Wal-Mart Supercenter. Danny spoke with the manager and he called LeAnn to the front. She followed us outside and sat on the bench next to the doors. I sat down beside her. Danny squatted on his heels in front us.

"LeAnn," Danny said. "Do you know a young man by the name of Mark Addison."

Her eyes lit up and she smiled.

"Yeah, he's my boyfriend."

"Have you seen him today?" he asked.

She shook her head. "He'll probably stop by tonight and then we'll drive around for a little while after I get off work. He doesn't come to the house much, daddy doesn't like him." She gave Danny a lopsided grin. "Daddy doesn't like any of the guys I've gone out with."

I looked Danny in the eye. He gave a slight shake of his head. I leaned back against the bench and watched.

"LeAnn, hon. Are you pregnant?"

LeAnn slumped forward and dropped her face in her hands.

"Oh, God. Who told you that?"

"It was just a guess."

"But...but, why?"

"Mark is dead, hon. Someone shot him."

"Nooooo," LeAnn wailed. "No, no, no, no. I should have never told mama. I knew she would tell him. Oh, God. Mark and I should have just waited until he finished school and ran away."

Tears coursed down her cheeks. I put an arm around her and patted her back. I looked at Danny over her shoulder.

"I'll go tell the manager that LeAnn is going to have to leave early today. We'll give her a ride home."

I patted her back as she cried on my shoulder, then led her to the car and held the door as she slipped inside. Danny took the keys and started the car. I got in front and found some napkins in the door pocket. I passed them to the devastated girl. She was no longer crying, just staring at nothing.

"He can't tolerate gossip," she whispered once.

I wondered who she was talking about.

We pulled into the drive of a small neat house and parked behind a F350 Ford. Danny flipped off the headlights, but made no move to get out. LeAnn showed no sign of wanting to leave the car. I sat and waited to see what was going to happen next.

Danny picked up his cell phone and dialed.

"You get a hit on the prints we found in the room?" he asked. "Yeah, I'm there now." He paused to listen a minute. "No, Walker's here with me. We'll be fine."

He punched off the phone and dropped it on the seat.

"LeAnn, is your mother at home?"

She shook her head. "She's at work."

"Your dad still drinking?"

"Sometimes."

"You stay here in the car, okay?"

She nodded. Danny and I got out of the car. He knocked. We could hear the television through the door, but no one answered. Danny peeked through the window. No one was in the front room. I motioned toward the doorknob. Danny nodded. I reached out and it turned easily in my hand. I pushed it open a crack and Danny called out.

"Milt, you there? It's Danny Morton, we need to talk."

No answer, just the canned laughter from a sitcom soundtrack.

Danny loosed his nine millimeter from the holster on his hip and pushed through the door. I followed him in and we spread out. Danny called out from time to time, but didn't get any response. He moved into the kitchen. I opened the bedroom door. A man was slumped on the bed with a shotgun balanced between his legs. The wall behind him was splattered with blood and brain matter. I holstered my weapon and called to Danny. Mark's killer wasn't going to do any more harm.

# REJECTION

*L*isa's breath caught in excitement as she slipped the heavy cream-colored paper from the envelope. The embossed logo glittered in the sunlight as she flattened the paper on the table and started to read.

Dear Ms. Portleson,

I enjoyed your book, Talisman of the Tiger, very much. The characters were outstanding, the setting fantastic. I wanted to drop everything and stop by the guesthouse for a drink with your protagonist. The story was beautifully detailed and the ending an exquisite surprise.

Unfortunately, I do not believe my agency is the proper one to handle this property. Please don't feel badly about this rejection as there are many other agencies and I'm sure one of them will have the contacts necessary to place this excellent book.

Sincerely,

Liter A. Ryagent
Author Representative

"That's it!" She yelled, crumpling the cream-colored paper into a ball.

"I've had it. Agents are bastards and I am absolutely not going to get another, 'we love your book but we don't want to represent it' letters."

David rolled his eyes behind the sports page. "Calm down, Lis. It's not like the worlds gonna end if you don't sell your book."

"David, I'm warning you. Be gone."

"Baby, I thought we were gonna..."

"You thought wrong. Dammit, I'm having a crisis here and the nicest thing you could think of to say was, 'the worlds not gonna end if you don't sell your book.' GET OUT!"

The newspaper slapped onto the table as David rose from his chair.

"Jeez, Lis. You need to get some help."

"OUT!"

David slammed through the door. Lisa opened a bottle of wine.

\* \* \*

The tub overflowed with bubbles, a half-empty wine bottle balanced on the rim. Candles scented the room. Lisa turned on the hot tap. Water lapped over the sides and dripped onto the floor. She tipped the bottle for another drink and closed her eyes.

A few minutes later, a smile flickered across her face. Imagination was a wonderful thing. She could kill off every agent and publisher that ever rejected her books without ever getting out of the tub. Of course, she could get out of the tub. That was the beauty of imagination: you could take it anywhere. Why, it was even better than sex. The smile curved her lips once more and she lifted the bottle for a drink. Wine dribbled down her chin as she settled deeper into scented water.

The cat pawed a bloody shirt out of the laundry hamper. In the bedroom, flies buzzed around an inert figure. As the sun crept over the horizon, the candles smoked and guttered out. The New

York Times early edition lay in a soggy mess on the bathroom floor. Literary Agent Murdered! Screamed the headlines. Lisa sighed and pondered the 22-point type as she drained the last of the wine. Imagination really was a wonderful thing.

# New mystery by kd easley in stores now!

# kd easley

Author, kd easley, is a union carpenter who spends her downtime in Missouri trying to keep two psycho cats from tap dancing on her keyboard while she's trying to write.

Get to know kd at www.kdwrites.com where she shares information about upcoming books, writer's conferences and resources, and blogs about writing, life, and living with crazy felines.

www.ingramcontent.com/pod-product-compliance
Lightning Source LLC
Chambersburg PA
CBHW020634130626
46552CB00003B/1227